These tales belong to:

....

....

Tales from a Tall Forest

Tales From a Tall Forest
published in 2017 by
Hardie Grant Egmont
Ground Floor, Building 1, 658 Church Street
Richmond, Victoria 3121, Australia
www.hardiegrantegmont.com

A CiP record for this title is available from the National Library of Australia.

Design and typesetting by Pooja Desai

3 5 7 9 10 8 6 4 2

Printed in China through Asia Pacific Offset

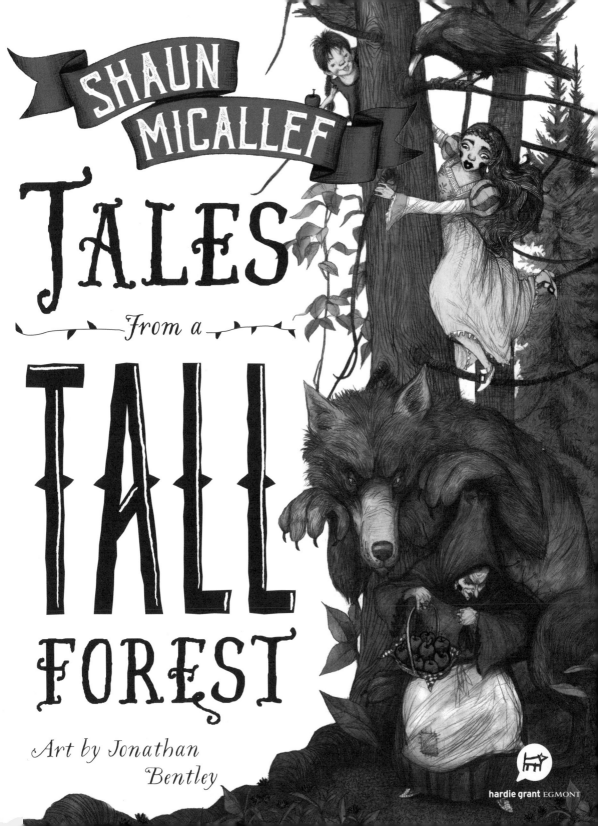

SHAUN MICALLEF

TALES from a TALL FOREST

Art by Jonathan Bentley

hardie grant EGMONT

For Judy and Fred.

– S.M

For Maripaz, Harvey and Ruby.

– J.B

CONTENTS

BEGIN

the

BEGINNING

Once upon a time being there was –

A piece of wood!

No, no, my children. Once upon a time being there were *a number of pieces of wood*. A forest. But not just any forest; this was the LARGEST forest in all of Europe (which is where it was). The oldest, too. It was said that old King Pangloss himself planted the first seedling way back in 800 AD when he was passing through to visit the Pope. It was a beautiful forest as well – beautiful and WILD and full of birds and animals, too many to be recorded. And running through the middle of the forest was a babbling brook fed from a tumbling waterfall high atop a mountain on which sat, like an ancient lion, a splendid castle called Tancred.

From the old King's small labour (when he was young) grew the mighty forest over which Tancred stood sentry. In fact, Tancred watched over not only the forest but the whole valley and the many lands beyond which made up the kingdom.

And the old King had ruled over it all for as long as anyone could remember. And because the old King was a very wise and good man, his subjects called him King Pangloss the Sanguine (which means 'cheerful', although nobody knew that) and put it about that he ruled with a fist of velvet.

But, because he was also a strong king, history tells that it was a fist of velvet wrapped in a gauntlet of STEEL.

Now, children, you may be thinking to yourselves, 'But I thought this was going to be a book about a forest. After all, you've called it *Tales from a Tall Forest* and there is a picture of a forest on the cover,' and this is true. It IS a story about a forest and all the things that went on in it – AND the woodsman who looked after it. But you must be patient. We will get to all that in a moment.

Now, in the early days King Pangloss had no trouble ruling over his kingdom, mainly because there weren't very many people in it to rule. People died young and often back then and if they were lucky enough to survive into adulthood, they'd usually be so grateful that they'd happily do almost anything they were told. But after the terrifying and awful bubonic plague was over, towards the latter part of the olden days, there were a lot more people about because people weren't dying so often. And these people began to notice that sometimes their neighbours had more milking stools and rat traps and scythes than they did, and this bred a certain amount of discontent. You see, jealousy, envy and greed were new feelings and no-one knew quite how to handle them.

King Pangloss was overwhelmed by the amount of disputes that needed settling, so he decreed a number of laws to protect the rights of some of the people and punish the wrongs of others. He also appointed a Sheriff to oversee these new laws so he didn't have to worry about them anymore.

The new Sheriff was a fine gentleman by the name of Belknap. He was fair and just and used the money he collected in taxes to improve the lands of the rich people – now called 'nobles' – who would, in turn, use the rent from their tenants – now called 'peasants' – to pay their taxes. It was a good system and worked well until the peasants realised what was going on, decided they wanted no part of it and instead went to live in the forest, which, while part of the King's personal domain, was so large and

deep and thickly wooded that the Sheriff's men could spend their whole lives searching and find not a single soul.

In the nooks and crannies or high atop old trees or in burrows and underground caverns, the people made their homes. They lived off the bounty of the forest, picking its fruit and trapping animals for food and clothing, or for training as beasts of burden. Some opened market stalls or plied their trades in small businesses, but most hid themselves and lived quietly away from any trouble.

Only one of the King's men knew his way around the forest with any skill or certainty: THE ROYAL WOODSMAN. Every morning before the sun rose he would leave the palace to fetch wood for the castle's many fireplaces and furnaces or to cut down timber for the Royal Furniture Makers or the Royal Builders. He would, from time to time, come across a peasant family or group of dwarves who had built their dwellings from the King's trees but, providing they only used what they needed

– and left alone certain trees (like the spruce and the birch and the larch and the oak and the maple and the poplar and the cedar and the fig and the banyan and the endangered Scots pine and the rare Irish Yew and, of course, the almost certainly non-existent Patagonian Bonsai Ficus) – he did not bother reporting them to the Sheriff and they, in return, let him go about his business. Sometimes he'd even advise them about which wood to use for their houses or how to cut it, even which berries they should or shouldn't eat or how they must never lay traps for the animals, as this was forbidden.

Except for the rats. No-one liked rats.

The peasants who lived in the forest were nice but very gullible and were likely to believe anything the Woodsman told them. The Royal Woodsman was the highest-born person they knew. To amuse himself now and then, the Woodsman would warn the peasants, in a solemn voice, to stay away from 'The Enchanted Glade'. Of course, there was no such thing as 'The Enchanted Glade' but it did mean that that section of the woods, where he kept his shed and stored his timber and tools, would be left alone. Of course, when the peasants learnt of an Enchanted Glade, they were very curious and, while they didn't have the courage to visit the area for very long, they would gather around its edges with a giddy mix of excitement and fear, and imagine they saw some magical occurrence. They often returned home with amazing tales of talking wolves or pigs that could build things, of whispering wells, and all manner of wondrous strange.

Born of hysteria, hallucinogenic toadstools and outright lies, a folklore grew like Topsy about the forest and these stories were told and retold in endless variations.

The Royal Woodsman didn't feel too guilty about starting all this; after all, it made what would have otherwise been a very dull and boring life MUCH more interesting.

Everyone knew and loved the Royal Woodsman. Brothers Hengest and Hors, for example. They were two of the smartest peasants in the land and had started a business together in the forest. In exchange for three silver coins they would build you a barn or, for six, a house. Their preferred building material was wood but sometimes, when the Royal Woodsman felt they were using too much, they would switch to stone or thatch together reeds and cover the construction in river mud, which, when dry, could prove quite hardy. And THIS is where our story really starts —

The WOLF and the Princess and the TRAIL OF CRUMBS

The building business was booming but Hengest and Hors were getting a bit sick of building the same thing over and over again, so they were very, VERY interested when an old crone stopped by their dwelling with plans to construct a cottage made entirely of confectionary.

The old crone went by the name of Baba Yaga and she was a recent arrival. Hengest didn't recognise her accent but Hors thought she might have been Trebizondian.

'You'll have to build it under the ledge of a cliff,' said Hengest, looking at her drawings. He was concerned about the colours running if it rained. Hors was more worried about the ants.

It was, it must be said, a sweet little cottage with liquorice-allsort stones, candy-cane door frames and a rooftop of chocolate pieces all grouted together with marzipan. The garden had trees of musk sticks crowned with peppermint leaves and there was a darling little path made of sprinkles that went all the way around the house to a small ornamental pond of ginger ale, which was constantly refreshed by a sherbet fountain. All of that was do-able and exciting; what worried Hengest and Hors was the massive walk-in oven in the kitchen.

That, and the cages.

'For the children,' explained the old crone. 'That's why they don't have to be full-size and I save money.'

Hengest and Hors were still worried. Perhaps even more so.

'Although they can't be TOO small,' she continued, 'because they need to accommodate the children as they become fatter and fatter.'

One of them had to say something. Neither of them saying anything didn't seem to be working.

'Are you intending to kidnap these children and cook them?' asked Hors as diplomatically as possible.

'Only to eat,' explained the old crone. 'I wouldn't dream of doing it just for sport. That'd be cruel.'

'Would you excuse us for a moment, Mrs Yaga?' said Hengest, grabbing Hors by the elbow and pulling him towards the door.

The brothers were in a bind. On the one hand they had a customer with an exciting new project, but on the other hand she was planning to use it to capture and eat small children.

'I've never worked with such challenging building materials,' said Hengest to Hors as they huddled in the alley to discuss the matter. 'The possibilities are endless.'

'Yes, but consider the cottage's use,' reasoned Hors, unconvinced by his brother's enthusiasm. 'Cannibalism has been against the law since the Great Famine ended in 1317.'

The two debated the pros and cons, form versus function, nutritional value over aesthetics. Meanwhile, the old crone, who had grown tired of waiting, wandered next door to Peatbog McGinty, the barn builder, and showed him her drawings. He had no problem with the idea of a candy slaughterhouse and would do it for half the price.

It was almost two and a half years before Baba Yaga moved into her new home – there had been delays getting certain permits and approvals from Sheriff Belknap – and by then the old crone was quite blind. This was to cause her a few problems when it came to child-catching and consuming – as we shall see (and she would not).

Meanwhile, back at the castle, the King was away on a skiing holiday in Münster. There was nothing he enjoyed more in the spring than to be towed along the Rhine by a Viking ship filled with a galley of madly paddling shield-maidens. Especially since his beloved wife, the Queen, had died of mange and his new Queen, though astonishingly beautiful, had a heart of pitiless stone and was not much fun to be around. In fact, she made life in the royal household most unpleasant for everyone, especially the young princesses – and extra-specially for the youngest princess, Mathilda.

Mathilda was quite a beauty in her own right. She had skin as white as alabaster, lips as red as blood, and hair as black as a raven's wing.

These days, of course, such contrasts are commonplace – but you have to remember that in the olden days, dyes and cosmetics were very uncommon and so Mathilda was considered quite breathtakingly attractive.

Vanity, though, has always been with us and Mathilda's wicked stepmother, the new Queen, would sit for hours in front of her mirror brushing her hair and practising her smiles.

She had many smiles: the Surprised Smile, the Delighted Smile, the Indulgent Smile, the Understanding Smile, the Naughty Smile, the Sympathetic Smile. But her favourite was probably the Lovely Smile, a smile that seemed to shine from the purest of hearts but, really, was the result of much practice and tight muscle control. Not that it was just about the mouth – the Lovely Smile was as much about the angle of the head and the promise of a joyful laugh, the crinkle at the top of her nose, and the way her hair played about her shoulders when her head turned. Oh, it was about many things, but the key to the Lovely Smile was the illusion of its bespokeness: that were it not for you, there would be no Lovely Smile at all. It was for you and only you – and it was this Lovely Smile that she trained on the reflection of her stepdaughter like a crossbow as Mathilda entered the room.

Though not without her beauty, the Queen was, shall we say, a little *pointy* – her chin and nose especially – but from certain angles and when the light was right, she could be quite stunning. Alongside the effortless beauty of the young Princess, though, the forty-something stepmother seemed posed and careful, and her eyes could not help but flash a lustrous envy as the Princess drew close behind her.

'You called for me, Stepmother?' asked the Princess, bobbing a respectful curtsey.

'I did, Mathilda,' said the Queen with an Extra-Lovely Smile as she continued brushing her hair. 'I'm worried for you, my dear.'

'Worried? For me?' The Princess wrinkled her brow, which – amazingly – made her look even more beautiful. This was not lost on the Queen.

'Yes,' replied the Queen. 'You look as pale as a snow-drift, child. I think you should get out in the sunshine for the day. Maybe go for a little walk in the woods.'

The Princess liked the idea of going for a walk but her father, the King, had forbidden his daughters from ever venturing outside the castle, for fear they would be set upon and harmed by some of his less-worthy subjects. Too poor to live even in a hollowed-out tree and forage for nuts, many lived off the refuse tossed over the walls by Tancred's monks and had set up shanties and lean-tos along the eel-infested moat. Dressed in rags and matted in filth, they huddled together for most of the day,

warming themselves by the burning globs of pitch the turret guards would sometimes drop upon them out of mercy. Their only respite from the misery was to fight over food scraps, play in the hourly discharge of castle effluent[1] or attack their betters (of whom there were many). The prospect of waylaying a Princess as she crossed the drawbridge would have been irresistible. It was their way of letting King Pangloss know that not everyone in his kingdom loved him.

[1] A kind of toilet water.

'Oh, nonsense,' said the Queen, swivelling from the mirror to face the Princess and realising that the girl was even more beautiful in the flesh than by reflection. 'Your father is being far too cautious. You're a growing girl – how old are you now?'

'Fifteen, ma'am.'

'Almost a woman,' laughed the Queen through her Lovely Smile. 'Why, when I was your age, I was living by myself in a tower right in the *very middle* of a forest.'

'Oh?' said the Princess. In truth, she had grown bored of the castle and longed to see the real world.

'Of course, my hair was much longer than yours,' laughed the Queen again, playfully tapping her stepdaughter's perfectly upturned nose with a powder-puff. 'But the views were wondrous to behold and it was there I met my very first husband.'

'Really?' said the Princess, incredulous that the prospect of romance might be within the reach of someone as young as she.

'Of course,' chirruped the Queen, being careful to

angle her head into the light so that her pointiness was to her advantage. 'Sadly, I tarried too long in the tower and by the time I was banished, my poor husband-to-be –'

'A prince?' asked the Princess eagerly. (She did *love* the idea of princes.)

'The most handsome of princes,' the Queen assured her. 'But the very day I was sent off to make my way in the world, my beloved fell from the tower for one reason or another and was blinded by some thorns.'

The Princess's own eyes welled up with tears, producing quite a remarkable effect. The light, which the Queen had laboured over with admirable geometric skill to favour herself, now glinted with glorious happenstance on the impossibly big blue eyes of the Princess, creating a sparkling gossamer veil through which her now almost incandescent beauty could just be glimpsed, thus making the experience of looking at her akin to being engulfed by some dazzling heavenly vision of loveliness – which, of course, just made the Queen keener to get rid of her.

'But eventually we found each other in the woods

by singing to each other,' the Queen reassured the girl, patting her on her perfect, milk-white arm, 'and we lived happily ever after.'

'Until you met Daddy,' the Princess reminded her.

'My point is that a walk in the woods will do you good,' said the Queen, her Lovely Smile being tested. 'You are very pasty, my dear.'

'But surely I will be in the shadows, were I to walk in the woods,' reasoned the Princess. 'If I were to walk along the banks of the river, I would receive the full benefit of the sunbeams, plus the cooling effect of the breeze off the water —'

'No, it must be the woods,' insisted the Queen, perhaps a little too sharply.

The Princess blushed a little, which merely added to her prettiness in a strawberries-and-cream kind of way.

'What I mean is,' continued the Queen, stroking the girl's hand sweetly, 'that too much sun too soon might be too much for a girl of your complexion. Better that you be sun-dappled for your promenade than exposed to the full harshness of the rays as they beat unrelentingly upon you.'

The Princess nodded that she understood – and indeed she did, for she was no fool – but her fears were not mollified for she had heard all manner of terrible tales of what could befall the unwary should they enter the forest. Why, just last week a little curly blonde-haired girl had been eaten by bears, they said. The tyke had cut through the woods on her way home from a maypole lesson, lost her way and ended up in a cave near Scrapefoot's Bog. All Sheriff Belknap's men found when they kicked down the door was a shambles of shattered furniture, unmade beds and some porridge. No trace of the little girl.

Yet still the Queen insisted. The young and extraordinarily beautiful Princess would be accompanied by the Queen's very own tall, strong and handsome Royal

Huntsman, she promised. He was adept with a bow, knew the woods like the back of his dagger-filled hand and could dispatch a wild animal with the unseeable speed of a whip-crack. If anyone could protect the unwary as they ventured through the forest it was the trusty, dead-eyed, heavily weaponed behemoth they called the Royal Huntsman.

Unfortunately, he was off with a cold and so the Royal Woodsman was summoned instead.

The Royal Woodsman was highly chuffed to be chosen as the young Princess's chaperone. He knew every thicket, clump, spinney, dingle and grove of the forest in even greater detail than the Royal Huntsman, who merely hid behind the trees as he went about his work; for the Royal Woodsman, the trees WERE his work. He could look after himself in a tight spot. He knew his way around a kindling knife and had seen off more than a few badgers and shrews in his time. Once, he even ran away from an otter! No, the woods were perfectly safe if you knew what to look out for or which tree to hide up. Dutch elms were the best: strong, sturdy and with big wide branches to hang off. He was sure Princess Mathilda would come to no harm in his care.

So he was more than a little puzzled when the Queen took him to one side and said she also wanted her stepdaughter's heart cut out and brought back in a jewellery box.

'I'm sorry, your Majesty, I didn't quite catch that,' he said, eyelids hammering.

The Queen looked over at the Princess, who was playing a harpsichord divinely on the other side of the room. 'She is too beautiful to live,' whispered the Queen, quietly dumping out the contents of her own jewellery box on the dressing table and handing it to the Woodsman.

The Woodsman scarcely knew what to say – which was just as well, because it wasn't his place to argue. She was the Queen and he was just a lowly tradesman. His job was to do as he was bidden. Plus, she had a lovely smile. The Royal Woodsman had lost his wife to croup a year ago and was a sucker for a lovely smile. They set a date for tomorrow.

As it turned out, though, tomorrow was going to be a particularly difficult day for the Royal Woodsman, perhaps the most particularly difficult day he had ever had. Not only did he now have to slay a princess in the forest, but as a single parent he first had to get his own children off to school. It was a new school, too, and he was worried they wouldn't be able to find their way home. He didn't want the same fate to befall them as befell that little curly blonde-haired child he'd heard about.

As the Royal Woodsman dropped off his children at Dame Gothel's Maypole Academy, he wiped the tears from their eyes (and his own too) and explained that they should have no trouble making their way back through the forest to their house that evening as he had torn up their lunch on the way to school, leaving them a trail of breadcrumbs to follow. He warned them not to talk to strangers or stray from the path, and told Hansel to look after his sister, even though she was five years older. He kissed them both, explained that he might be late home and not to be alarmed if he had a bit of blood on him. Gretel hugged him one more time and he waved them goodbye as he set off for the palace.

Princess Mathilda was dressed and ready and as excited as she could be. Radiant and glowing and vibrant and all but bursting with joy and beauty and love, she skipped about, gathering up her butterfly net and hoop and picnic things and sun hat and favourite doll, singing a pretty song as she went (she had a sweet voice, which surprised no-one). All ready, she hugged her stepmother goodbye and slipped her hand into the worried-looking Royal Woodsman's, looking up at him with such unalloyed trust it would have very nearly broken his heart there and then had she not dragged him away, blowing kisses all the while to her seething stepmother.

'Bye-bye, my darling,' cooed the Queen with a tight wave and a final blast of her loveliest Lovely Smile.

Try as they might, the woods could be nothing other than delightful. The Royal Woodsman may have trudged along in silence, wondering how on earth he was to carry out his dreadful errand, but the young Princess – running ahead and *ooh*-ing and *aah*-ing at the most

everyday of things – was oblivious. Shards of light
would catch her as she turned and giggled at various
flowers and mice and tree-roots, pointing them out and
looking back, her trusting face filled with wonder. She
asked a flurry of questions at such speed that the sullen
Woodsman could not have possibly answered them even
if he had wanted to. Her amazement and naiveté and
spinning as the light caught her created a kaleidoscope
of innocence that would have charmed even the wildest
of forest creatures.

Deer and squirrel, coaxed from their timidity, joined
fox and stoat to watch the beautiful Princess twirl,
giggling and *la-la-la*-ing, until she fell, exhausted,
laughing and dizzy, on a clump of lichen.

The Royal Woodsman swatted a gnat buzzing about his neck and knelt down to adjust his sock, surreptitiously removing the dagger secreted in his garter. He wanted to be home before dark to make his children dinner: ham hocks in honey and rhubarb. Gretel loved honey and rhubarb; she was a sucker for anything sweet. Hansel, too. Thoughts of his children played vividly in his head as he stepped towards the Princess, who was kneeling at the edge of a pond, talking to a frog on a lily pad.

'Do you think he's really a handsome prince, Mr Woodsman?' asked the girl enchantingly.

'No, Your Highness, no,' said the Royal Woodsman, quickly tucking the knife up into the sleeve of his jerkin so she couldn't see. 'That's a frog. A handsome prince would be much more ... handsome and princely –'

'No, no, silly,' laughed the Princess with a bewitching guilelessness that bordered on perfection. 'I mean, what if I *kissed* him to break the spell? Perhaps then he would turn into a handsome prince.'

'I wouldn't be kissing any frogs around here, Your Highness,' warned the Royal Woodsman as he stood over her. 'Very dangerous.'

Mathilda looked at the frog. 'Dangerous?' she said, unable to believe that something so cute and green and funny could possibly cause her any harm.

'Oh, yes,' said the still-looming Woodsman.

The frog ribbited and the Princess let out a giggle. She couldn't see what the frog saw: the woodsman raising his dirk on high, the blade glinting in the light as a breeze parted the leaves above him.

'He seems perfectly harmless to me,' said the Princess, still hopeful the frog might be a prince, and a handsome one at that.

Ribbit, ribbit ...

'Chytrid fungus,' said the Royal Woodsman, sweat beading on his brow. 'It's sweeping through the amphibious population 'round these parts. I wouldn't be kissing any of them if I were you.'

'Oh, poo,' said the Princess.

The frog hopped from the lily pad into the pond and swam away. When the Princess turned to the Woodsman, he was sitting on a rock with his head in his hands.

'Oh dear,' said the Princess, rushing to the man's side to comfort him. 'Whatever can be the matter, Royal Woodsman? May I know?'

Princess Mathilda was so wonderful and sweet and charming (and beautiful) that he knew he could never carry out the Queen's wishes. What would his children think? His late wife would certainly not approve. And he believed in a God – and a God would surely rain down the most dreadful vengeance upon him were he to take the life of so angelic a creation as the Princess. No, no – he would have to think of something else. Perhaps the Princess would be able to help; she was, after all, high born and presumably possessed of some wisdom, if not actual education. He explained his dilemma.

The Princess listened intently to the Woodsman's tale of near treachery. At first she found the whole thing inconceivable. She had grown up in a cocoon of love and warmth and joy; that the human heart was capable of such blackness was so foreign a notion to her that she could barely make out the meaning of the words in the order the Woodsman was saying them. She stared, bug-eyed (but still lovely), as the Royal Woodsman tried to make himself understood. The Queen was jealous of her. *Why?* Because you are so beautiful. *Me, beautiful?* Yes, have a look at your reflection in the pond. *My reflection?* Yes, the image of yourself thrown back to you by a body of water or other light-refractive surface. *Oh, yes, I see.* Well, that's the trouble. *But why would she want me dead?* Because you are more beautiful than she is. *More beautiful?* Yes, look in the pond again. *Oh, right – yes, I see.* You're a threat to her. *I understand. How very sad.* Yes, it is sad, Your Highness. *I'm very beautiful, aren't I?* Yes, you are. Plus, you're younger, which just makes it worse. *Really? She's threatened by that as well?* I'm afraid so. *Oh ...*

The Princess had never thought of herself as beautiful before and the realisation of it changed her forever. She lost something of her innocence that day by the pond and, in a cosmic injustice that regrettably is the stuff of life, the young Princess would never be quite as enchantingly lovely as she was before she had her enchanting loveliness pointed out to her. The witless would be quick to call that 'irony' – but it was sadder than that.

about to set off when
through some bushes ran
a terrified little girl in what
looked like a red poncho.

'My grandmother!
My grandmother!' cried
the little girl.

'What's happened?'
asked the Princess.

'A wolf has eaten her,'
exclaimed the little girl,
out of breath from all
the running she had
done. 'I could hear her
yelling from inside his
stomach –'

'Gosh,' exclaimed
the Princess.

'Hold on,' said
the Woodsman.

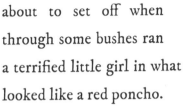

'You heard yelling from *inside* the wolf's stomach?'

The little girl nodded.

'Are you saying your grandmother is still *alive?*'

The girl continued nodding. She was leaning up against a tree, panting as the Princess rubbed her wrists to calm her.

'So the wolf didn't *bite* her or *tear her to pieces* as he ate her? He just swallowed her whole?' the Woodsman pressed her. It didn't really make sense.

'Royal Woodsman, can't you see the poor girl is distressed?' scolded the Princess, with a crossness that was quite becoming.

'Begging Your Highness's pardon, but it sounds more like a *python* has eaten her grandmother than a wolf –'

'Oh, no, it was a wolf, all right,' said the little girl. 'He bit the hood off my coat as I ran out.' She displayed the back of what turned out not to be her poncho after all. Her coat was torn and ripped and still had saliva on it.

'How big was this wolf?' the Woodsman asked, inspecting the damage with some concern.

'Well, he was big enough to fit into my grandmother's nightdress,' explained the girl, standing on her tiptoes and holding her arm up at full stretch to indicate the height of the beast as best she could. As she was very small, this didn't help create an accurate picture.

It was the Princess's turn to be dubious. 'Why was he wearing your grandmother's nightdress?' she asked.

'He was *disguised* as my grandmother,' explained the little girl. 'I brought over a basket of shopping for her because she's been poorly, only to find –'

'Does your grandmother *look* anything like a wolf?' Princess Mathilda asked.

'It's a very dark room. I mean, he was in the bed with the quilt pulled up under his chin –'

'But he's a wolf. Surely the snout and the fangs and the fur –'

'Well, it had been some time since I'd seen her –'

'But surely the growling would have –'

'And the paws!'

'Look, the wolf could talk, all right?' said the little

girl impatiently. 'I was suspicious, sure. Who wouldn't be? I asked her a few questions and by the time the penny dropped, it was too late. I was lucky to get out of there with my head still on. Now, are you going to help me get my grandmother out of his stomach or what?'

Princess Mathilda stood knock-kneed and helpless and quite adorable in a newborn-foal kind of way. Of course, none of this was at all helpful in the circumstances.

The Royal Woodsman reached into the leather sling behind him and produced a gleaming stave-handled axe with a bearded Frankish head. Had she pearls, the Princess would have clutched them. 'Lead the way to Grandma's house, Tiny Poncho Girl,' he demanded. Perhaps they wouldn't have to buy an ox heart after all.

Through the forest they raced, past Donlevy's Cave at the foot of Dunphy Hill, on by the old Bodkin place, Wizard's Glen, the practice tree of Torino the Archer, around the Dark Wood of Caliphy (too scary to cut through), across the bridge over the Voltonian Sulphur Lakes and very quickly under the Haunted Caves of Arkadian via a series of intricate tunnels. They even happened past Hengest and Hors, who were inspecting what appeared to be a pile of straw, a pile of sticks and some sort of pigsty made of kiln-fired mud bricks. The two brothers were talking with three wild boars about acts of God and insurance and when warned by the Woodsman, the Princess and Tiny Poncho Girl that there was a wolf on the loose, the wild boars became even wilder and began squealing and pointing and making wind-whistling noises. Hengest and Hors tried to settle them as our trio bade their adieus and continued on their way, but there was no calming them.

Soon enough, the three arrived at Grandma's house.

It was deathly quiet but for the sound of some light snoring inside. The little girl adjusted her poncho and pushed open the door, gesturing that the others should enter before her. The Woodsman wasn't sure what the Royal protocol was and made a similar gesture to the Princess. The Princess shook her head and gestured that he go in ahead of her. 'After all,' she whispered, 'you've got the axe.'

Our heroes sneaked in with great stealth so as not to wake the sleeping wolf, who was tucked up as neat as you please in a charming little canopied bed with a coverlet over him and his head resting on a lovely silk-tasselled pillow covered in embroidered unicorns. His mouth was hanging open, his tongue lolled out and his foul breath reeked of undigested grandmother.

'Help! Help!' cried a muffled voice from inside him. Using all his skills as the kingdom's finest axeman, the Royal Woodsman gently carved open the belly of the wolf and, still being very careful not to disturb his slumber, helped the elderly woman step out. There was obviously a lot of blood but she was so grateful to be rescued, she didn't seem to mind that her sheets and eiderdown had been completely ruined. As the woman silently hugged her granddaughter, the Princess couldn't help noticing that she, while no oil painting, looked NOTHING like a wolf. Perhaps the little girl needed eye glasses, she thought. She would write her a letter of introduction to Tommaso de Modena, the Royal Spectacle Maker, when time allowed, and maybe spring for some nice frames.

Right now, though, they had a bisected animal to dispose of and that was a tricky business. All the creatures of the forest – the King's domain – belonged to the King and poachers were heavily frowned upon (unless they were catching rats). In fact, the penalty for catching a single fish in the babbling brook fed from the tumbling waterfall atop the mountain that Castle Tancred sat upon was five hundred lashes and a beheading. Goodness knows what would happen to you for slaughtering so proud a beast as a wolf, even a ravenous grandmother-eating one.

The grandmother suggested leaving the body where it was. She had a spinning wheel and could sew the wolf back together. 'Perhaps the Sheriff will think the wolf died in its sleep,' she suggested.

The Woodsman, in the process of placing the wolf's heart into the Queen's jewellery box, shook his head. 'A wolf dressed in a nightie with a scar that long is bound to raise questions. If there's an autopsy, there's no way they'll think it's natural causes. They'll match the wound to my axe and then it's only a matter of time before the Queen

figures this heart here doesn't belong to the Princess.'

'What about if we make it look like an accident?' suggested the Princess with a bright, engaging smile. Her teeth were as perfect as the keys on the organ in the Our Lady of Antwerp cathedral.

'Yes – an accident,' agreed Tiny Poncho Girl. 'Grandma wears the wolf like a coat, right? And she goes walking up the road to the bluff –'

'Singing a loud song –' added Princess Mathilda, gaily.

'Oh, yes,' agreed Tiny Poncho Girl, snapping her fingers. 'Singing a VERY loud song so as to attract everyone's attention.'

'"Sumer Is Icumen In",' suggested the Princess. It was her favourite. She'd played it the previous day on the harpsichord for her stepmother – and quite beautifully, too.

'So everyone is looking up at her on the bluff singing "Sumer Is Icumen In",' riffed the little girl, imagining the scene around her. 'And then she throws herself off the bluff and – SPLAT!!! – people will think that the wolf slipped and fell to his death on the rocks below and we've got all these witnesses.'

'Hang on a minute,' said the grandmother. 'That would involve me actually throwing myself off the bluff –'

'You'll be able to grab onto a branch on the way down,' explained the Princess.

'Yes,' added the little girl. 'And you could let the wolf's skin fall off you, you see – which would then slowly spiral down to the rocks below.'

'It's perfect,' cried Mathilda, clapping her hands and jumping up and down.

Grandma wasn't convinced. 'I'm eighty-seven years old. I can barely get out of bed in the morning. I'm not going to be able to hold on to some branch sticking out of a cliff.'

It was vexing.

'And why do *I* have to wear the dead wolf anyway?' complained the old woman.

'Because he *fits* you,' said the Princess, an exasperated tone creeping into her voice. Lovely, though ...

'He fits my *nightdress*,' Grandma corrected her.

'But you *look* like the wolf anyway,' added the little girl. 'It really is perfect.'

'I look NOTHING like the wolf,' protested the grandma. 'His ears, eyes and teeth are much bigger than mine; you told him so yourself –'

'The *wolf* looks like the wolf,' said the Woodsman quite sensibly. '*Anyone* can wear him.'

'But who WILL?' asked the old woman, still thinking she might have to.

Everyone looked at everyone else. Mathilda was the prettiest by far.

The Woodsman sighed and then made a small circle in the air with his finger, pointing at the others in the room as he recited a little rhyme to determine who would have to dress up:

'Rrrinspot,' he started. 'Vonza, twoza, zig-zag-zav, popti, vinaga, tin-li-tav. Harem, scarem, merchan, tarem, teir, tore –'

Suddenly the wolf stirred in the bed behind them.

The Woodsman, Tiny Poncho Girl, Princess Mathilda and Grandma raced out the door and through the forest as fast as they could go. Past Hengest and Hors, still arguing with the agitated boars, past the Haunted Caves of Arkadian, past the Voltonian Sulphur Lakes, past the Dark Wood of Caliphy, past the practice tree of Torino the Archer, past Wizard's Glen, past the old Bodkin place, past Donlevy's Cave at the foot of Dunphy Hill and even past the house of the Boy Who Cried Wolf (he wasn't home), with the wolf hot on their heels, holding together his rib cage, his jaws slavering, his big bad eyes wide and bloodshot and mad as could be (which was even more so now that he had no heart).

In their panic, the girl, the Princess, the old lady and the Woodsman became hopelessly lost but soon enough stumbled upon a trail of breadcrumbs. The Woodsman, ever keen of eye, recognised them instantly.

'These will lead to my cottage,' he said breathlessly. 'We can bar the doors and windows and will be as safe as safe can be.' (He was going to say 'safe as houses' but, having just seen what the wolf had done to the houses made of sticks and straw, he thought better of it.)

But the trail of breadcrumbs led only to Gretel and Hansel, who were in the process of following it from the other direction. The Royal Woodsman hugged his children and they all took refuge in a dense cluster of oak, beyond which lay Baba the Cannibal's Candy Slaughterhouse.

Through her spun-sugar window, old Baba's failing eyes could just make out a blurry blob running up the path of hundreds and thousands to her Rocky Road terrazzo porch. She hadn't eaten in days and was feeling faint but nonetheless quickly set the table and fired up the ovens. The blob had barely enough time to knock before she swung open the door and bade them enter.

'Come in, little ones,' she sang.

The band of six rushed in and the Royal Woodsman slammed and locked the door behind him. The old crone fetched some candy canes from the table behind her.

'You must be tired and hungry after your long journey. Now, how many of you are there?'

'There are several of us,' said the Princess, who was the first to get her breath back.

'Ooh – several of you, eh?' said Baba, smacking her lips. 'Who wants a candy cane?'

'Thank you, but there's no time for hospitality, ma'am,' interrupted the Woodsman as politely as he could. 'There's a wolf after us and we need to hide.'

'A wolf,' repeated Baba.

'Yes, a wolf,' re-repeated Grandma. 'He's already eaten me once and I don't want to be a second helping as well.'

Baba squinted at Grandma, trying to make her out. 'You don't sound like a *child*,' she said suspiciously.

'I never said I was,' said Grandma, helping herself to a candy cane anyway.

'There are children here, old woman,' confirmed the Woodsman, piling some chairs made of nougat in front of the door (made of hard toffee) and then checking out the window (spun icing sugar), 'and you're right, we need to ensure their safety first.'

'Well, I have some cages downstairs,' said Baba as innocently as she could, given what she was saying. 'They'd be perfectly safe in those.'

'A grand idea, old woman,' the Woodsman commended her. 'Princess Mathilda, take the children downstairs and see to it the crone locks you all in securely.'

'Oh, they'll never get out,' promised Baba, feeling along the wall for the door to the basement. 'Follow me, children.' She'd never eaten a princess before.

Mathilda herded together Hansel and Gretel and Tiny Poncho Girl and they all followed the strange old lady down the stairs while the Woodsman disappeared into the kitchen and pushed a heavy antique butterscotch sideboard up against the back door.

Meanwhile, back at Tancred, the Queen was growing restless. The Royal Woodsman had not yet returned with the Princess's heart and the sun was almost set. Tired of pacing backwards and forwards in front of her full-length mirror, she wrapped herself in a humble shawl and, armed only with a basket of poisoned apples, set out into the forest to do the job herself.

As the sun slipped behind the mountains, tendrils of night snaked their way through the woods, robbing Her Majesty of her beauteous pointiness. Plunged into shadow, with every pit and crag of her face lit from above by an unforgiving moon, the Queen resembled nothing less than the hag she was at heart.

The hamper of deadly fruit had been a gift from a jealous lover (Ardamanic of Scatera). It was destined for use as evidence in the young man's trial for High Treason, but the Queen thought she'd put it to much better use in her diabolical game of cat-and-mouse with the troublesome Princess. Little did she know that a far more ferocious player had entered the fray: one that would make both cat and certainly mouse seem tame by comparison. Ardamanic would ultimately be set free by the Lord Chamberlain for lack of proof, leaving him to bustle about once more in the world of come-hither-looks-over-fluttering-fans, but what the Queen had set in play by appropriating his poisonous cache of Granny Smiths would be remembered well after his naughtiness was nothing but a faded stain on the threadbare reputation of the so-called Aristocracy. But less of that later ...

Meanerwhile, the wolf had circled the ancient Trebizondian's House of Sweeties. Front door, back door, side door for the tradesmen, twelve windows, an aniseed drainpipe to shinny up, a hard caramel chimney to slide down and, on guard in the front yard, nothing more easily vanquished than three Marella jube garden gnomes with glacé cherry hats.

He gave the lollipop letterbox he was leaning on a
casual lick as he surveyed the building one more time. Pez
bricks and peanut brittle rendering – somewhere between
the solidity of a straw dwelling and a stick one, he guessed!

Certainly nowhere near possessing the structural integrity
of oven-baked clay and mortar. He could blow this one
down without too much difficulty, he thought.

Hengest and Hors and the three wild boars watched from behind a bush as the wolf drew a deep, deep breath – or, at least, attempted to. Because his lungs were disconnected from each other and hanging out of his open chest cavity, the wolf managed only to hyperventilate. Wheezing, he steadied himself on the lollipop letterbox and gathered up his intestines, using them to tie together his lungs and hold them in place. Once more, he tried to huff and puff the house down, but succeeded only in coughing his way into another near faint. No, he'd have to find another way of getting at his prey holed up inside and so, still holding his innards in, he stalked off back to his lair in the mountains to collect his thoughts.

Meanestwhile, inside Baba's Sugar Shack, the old crone was being the perfect hostess, serving double-fried chicken fat to the children in the cage and offering mild sedatives to the adults.

'No, thank you, old woman,' said the Woodsman. 'We must keep our wits about us if we're to thwart this ravenous wolf.'

'Yes, of course, dear,' Baba answered sweetly. 'But you're all so tense and these mandrake roots make for an excellent sleeping draught when dissolved in cormorant's blood.'

'It's *very* kind of you,' allowed the Woodsman, checking the window again, 'but to dull our senses would be exactly the *wrong* thing to do at this moment.'

'It's an extraordinarily powerful narcotic,' Baba sing-songed in what she hoped was an enticing key.

'No, thank you,' the Woodsman begged off.

'Can cause blurred vision, hallucinations, diarrhoea, vomiting, convulsions and excessive hair growth –'

'NO!'

Baba made a face even less pleasant than normal and proffered her tray of phials to Grandma, who was standing on a box on a chair near the front door, aiming a Byzantine fire-lance out of the transom. 'What about you, dearie? It's a member of the highly poisonous nightshade family –'

Grandma had one just to shut her up.

The door chime rang and the Royal Woodsman checked the peephole.

Outside was the unrecognisable Queen with a basket of apples. 'Fresh, delicious, free apples,' she called.

The Woodsman suspected it might be the wolf in disguise and so refused to open the door. Grandma agreed but also wanted to shoot the woman from the transom with the fire-lance. Baba also wanted whoever it was on the doorstep shot but mainly because giving away a healthy alternative like fruit door-to-door was a threat to her confectionary business.

But the Royal Woodsman wasn't so sure about *killing* the woman. There was something about the old woman's smile that seemed familiar to him. It was a lovely smile ... but before he could put two and two together, the real wolf – crudely sutured from his neck to his nethers by a terrified seamstress from nearby – sneaked up behind the old hag and devoured her whole.

At that same moment, however, Baba Yaga had pushed past the Woodsman and Grandma and swung open her front door to have words with the opportunist fruit vendor, only to find herself face to face with a slavering wolf. In this instance her poor vision was both a blessing and a curse: a blessing in that she couldn't see what dreadfulness was about to befall her and a curse in that, if she had, she might have been able to run away in time. But she couldn't and she didn't and she was gobbled up by the wolf as well.

Hengest and Hors and the three wild boars watched all this in horror and when the wolf, full of belly but empty of heart, skulked up the mountain to walk off his meal, they hightailed it back to the village to report all they had seen to Sheriff Belknap, who sent out several of his officers to ask questions, take notes and look important.

The Royal Woodsman and his children, along with Tiny Poncho Girl and her grandma, delivered the beautiful Princess to the dwarves' house for safekeeping – but to their surprise, the spare bed was already occupied by the little curly blonde-haired girl that everybody thought had been eaten by bears. She and Princess Mathilda ended up becoming great friends and, after the Princess was returned to the care and custody of the King, they would often meet and go frog-kissing in the woods together.

Tiny Poncho Girl ended up never growing up because, as it turned out, she was a faerie and would be forever small – but she got her glasses thanks to the Princess and never mistook her grandma for a wolf again. Grandma fell in love and married Ardamanic of Scatera, who, having changed his ways, was the perfect husband right up until her suspicious death less than three months later. He inherited everything.

The Royal Woodsman was knighted for his services to the Crown, and his children received lifelong peerages. Hansel now sits in the House of Lords and Gretel has written a spy novel.

The Sheriff's men eventually found what was left of the wolf. He had lost his way as he climbed the mountain that evening, and ended up falling off the bluff to his death on the rocks below (there were no branches to grab on the way down after all). He was eaten by bears.

Baba Yaga's house was condemned by the Department of Health and later also eaten by bears.

And the Princess's wicked stepmother – who had not only been eaten by a wolf but also been re-eaten by bears – was NEVER seen again.

❋

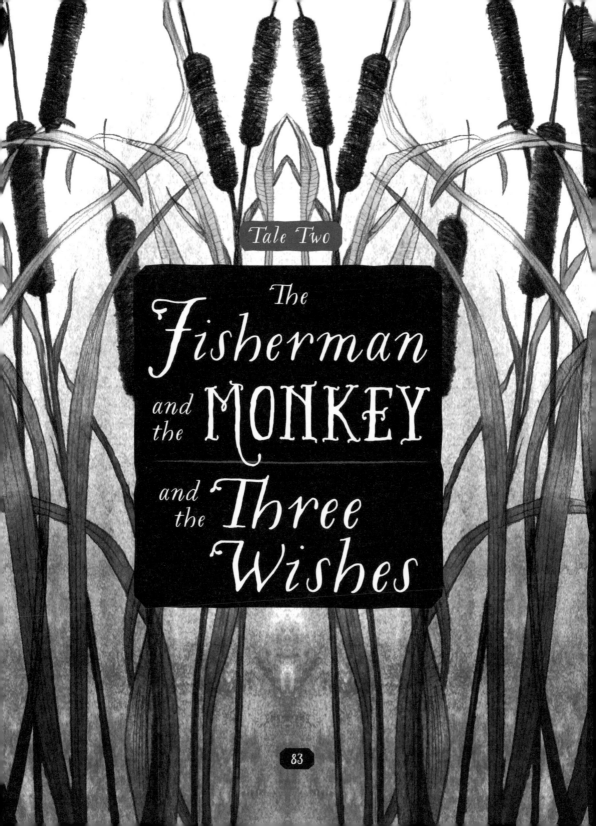

Tale Two

The Fisherman and the MONKEY and the Three Wishes

Forever and ever ago there was a fisherman and his wife. He had a fishing licence issued by Sheriff Belknap and would catch fish in the River Weser, and she ran her own market stall on the edge of the forest selling bundles of sticks tied together with gaily coloured ribbons. They were very happy together but didn't have any children.

'Oh, for a child,' said the wife one day upon returning home from a hard day's toil at the forest's edge. It had been a particularly good day, too, in which she managed to sell a particularly ugly bundle of sticks that had been sitting on the shelf for months and which she had been on the verge of throwing away. But the pleasure she would have otherwise derived from her daily work was always spoiled by coming home to a house where no son or daughter was waiting for her at the window.

The fisherman felt bad for his wife and wondered what he could do. Desperate to make her happy, he took up his fishing rod and tackle and went for a long walk along the river to think. Perhaps, he thought, he would find an abandoned child on the way and be able to take it home; he looked in the shrubs and reeds along the bank as he strolled by but found none. Maybe, he mused, he could carve one from a tree and somehow have it magically come to life – but no, tampering with nature like that always led to problems. What about, he pondered, if a small man made of gingerbread raced past with a thorn in his paw? If the fisherman removed the thorn, then surely the gingerbread man would agree to anything he wanted, like masquerading as a baby for the rest of his life. But no, no – he was clutching at straws.

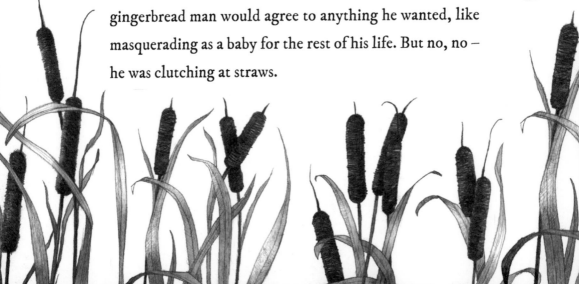

'Oh, for a REAL child,' he sighed as his wife had, casting out and hoping to at least snare a fish for their dinner.

'I can grant you that wish,' said a voice.

The fisherman looked about but saw no-one.

'Who's there?' he asked. He'd heard that the unwary were sometimes bewitched by water goblins at this hour. His neighbour, Old Bodkin, was said to have been transformed into a horse a few weeks ago by a magic pixie – though this later proved not so when Old Mrs Bodkin herself admitted to having pushed her husband off a cliff during an argument. The horse, it turned out, was just a horse.

Again, the voice spoke: 'If you wish to have a REAL child, you must grant me a favour in return.'

This time the fisherman saw from where the voice came. In a rowing boat on the river, only a little way from where he was fishing, was a monkey. Just a regular everyday monkey that you might see in a zoo, except, of course, this one could talk.

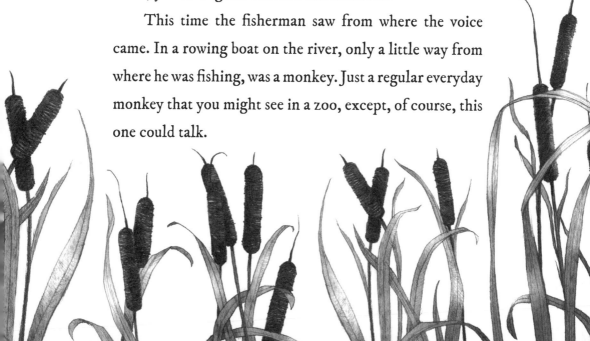

'A favour for a child,' said the monkey with a smile, which might have been charming had it been on a human.

The fisherman thought for a moment. It all sounded quite reasonable – a favour for a child – and just think how happy his wife would be!

'I agree,' said the fisherman, and the monkey rowed towards him.

The fisherman helped the monkey from the boat and they shook hands. The monkey's grip was powerful despite his small size. They sat down on a couple of tree stumps to work out the details.

The child would be a baby, they agreed. That way the fisherman and his wife could watch the child as it grew up and this would give them both great joy. Also, the child would be a boy and have blue eyes and blond hair. He'd be tall, too (later, of course, not while he was a baby). The fisherman wasn't sure whether the boy should have dimples or freckles and eventually settled on some of each.

Once the particulars of the child had been agreed upon, the fisherman stood to leave. It was getting late and his wife, who was a great worrier, would be worrying greatly about what had happened to him and imagining all sorts of terrible things. One time he had been tardy returning home from the fields by ten minutes or so and she had given him up for dead, tearfully sold all his things and rented out their house to a travelling pole-sitter while she moved into a nunnery; it had taken months to get rid of the pole-sitter as he was on his holidays and quite enjoyed sitting around in a comfortable home and not up a thirty-foot pole.

'Thank you, O Marvellous Monkey,' said the fisherman, shaking the monkey firmly by the paw. 'You have made me the happiest man in the kingdom.'

'But wait,' said the monkey. 'I haven't told you my favour.'

The monkey was right. In all his excitement about the child, the fisherman had completely forgotten his end of the bargain: the FAVOUR. He sat back down on the tree stump, crossed his legs, leant back, fell off, collected himself and sat back down again.

'What I would like,' said the monkey, tapping the fisherman on the knee with his huge, hairy finger, 'is for you to grant me THREE WISHES.'

This gave the fisherman pause. He was a simple man and had limited powers. He could tell a mackerel from a bream and empty a craypot. He could bait a hook with a maggot or harvest roe from a lumpfish if the seasons were with him, but beyond that he was – despite the reassurances of his kindly wife – next to useless. Still, the promise of a child proved too strong.

'I shall grant you whatever you wish, O Marvellous Monkey,' the fisherman assured the monkey with a chutzpah he'd never displayed before.

'THREE wishes,' stressed the monkey, holding up three long fingers.

'Of course, of course,' said the fisherman, imagining the look on his wife's face when he told her the good news. 'Whatever you want.'

When the fisherman returned home he found his wife already cradling a beautiful baby boy in her arms. He had never seen her so happy. Tears of joy were streaming down her face; her smile was beatific and joy was radiating from her every pore. She had never looked more lovely.

He didn't tell her about
the monkey.

Years passed – as they have a tendency to do – and the beautiful baby boy grew into a tall and handsome young man. He was in the barn tending to the oysters and the fisherman was on his knees in the house scrubbing the kitchen floor – as he always did when his wife was at work, even though she told him he needn't bother and that she'd do it when she got home – when he heard a knock at the door. Plopping his sponge back in the bucket, the fisherman walked into the front parlour, wiping his hands on his trousers as he went. Opening the door, he found the monkey standing there.

The fisherman had known this day would come but had been praying that it would not. So many years had gone by that he thought, just perhaps, that the monkey might have forgotten about the whole thing. Just in case, the fisherman had taken to avoiding the river in case he ran into the monkey. This he regretted because his son had often asked him to take him fishing and he always had to say no. But now the monkey had called anyway.

The fisherman invited the monkey in and offered him a chair by the fire. The monkey clambered onto it and warmed his big hands in the glow of the crackling flames. They exchanged pleasantries for a while, the fisherman distracted and hoping his son would not come in from the barn.

'You know why I am here, don't you?' asked the monkey, after the chitchat was exhausted.

The fisherman nodded. 'Your wish,' he said.

'My FIRST wish,' said the monkey, wagging his longest finger.

'Oh, yes, of course,' said the fisherman. 'What's it to be, O Marvellous Monkey?'

The fisherman held on to the slim possibility that the monkey – being a monkey – was going to ask for something simple like an apple or, at worst, nothing more complicated than a banana.

'I wish to have a hundred thousand gold sovereigns,' he announced, clasping his hands, smiling and closing his eyes as if he could see the coins already heaped before him.

The fisherman nodded his head slowly, blinking. A half-smile of his own was frozen on his face.

'And I want them within a week,' added the monkey, with another wag of his finger.

'Oh, yes, of course,' said the fisherman, as if it would be the easiest thing in the world.

The monkey tipped the brim of an imaginary hat and scampered out the window and up a tree, disappearing just as the fisherman's son walked in carrying two pails filled with clams.

'Is everything all right, Father?' asked the son, seeing his father's grave look.

'Yes, yes,' the fisherman lied. 'Things could not be better.'

That night the fisherman's wife was woken from her sleep by the sound of her husband in the next room counting out their savings. They had eight farthings. She gently chided him for worrying himself about money and tucked him back into bed. But he couldn't sleep. He lay there next to his soon-again-sleeping wife and worried himself all night.

The next day, he rose early and made his way down to Donlevy's Cave. Donlevy was an old dwarf and a miser who, in his eighty or so years, had never spent a single penny of what he had earnt during his lucrative career as Town Crier. He had retired many years ago and lived alone in a cave at the craggy foot of Dunphy Hill. He had no wife or children and no need for all the money that, legend had it, was hidden under his bed. MILLIONS, they said. Why, he dressed in rags and ate only the wild turnips his mangy dog would occasionally bring in, washing them down with the water that collected at the base of the damp walls of his cave.

He wouldn't miss a few gold coins.

Donlevy was not in. Probably down at the waterfall, guessed the fisherman, where the old dwarf would sometimes visit to wash himself if he was particularly filthy. The fisherman pushed open the battered door and went inside.

Donlevy's bed was small (as dwarf beds almost always are) and easily shifted. Underneath was a huge chest with a cheap lock (as miser's locks almost always are) and the fisherman had no difficulty snapping it open with his strong, work-hardened hands. Inside the chest was a glittering treasure of untold riches. Not only gold coins, but silver goblets and plates, and jewels of inestimable worth. All adding up far more in value than the rumoured MILLIONS, and much, much more than the fisherman believed possible for one man (particularly such a small man) to possess. Donlevy would never miss a mere hundred thousand gold coins.

And so the fisherman took them.

If Donlevy ever noticed – and it was said he counted his money by the moonlight every night – he never mentioned it. Perhaps his sight was failing; he was, after all, very old. The fisherman would leave the miser a basket of kippers outside his cave every week from then on – and sometimes some of his wife's delicious catberry strudel. He did so out of guilt but Donlevy thought the fisherman did so out of friendship and was forever thanking him. This made the fisherman feel even more guilty. The fisherman's wife, who knew nothing of what was going on, was merely puzzled when the dwarf stopped her and her husband in the street and thanked them profusely, sometimes weeping with gratitude. He even once offered to dress up in his old Town Crier costume and announce their twenty-fifth wedding anniversary to the citizenry. The fisherman's wife thought the old miser sweet but, out of an abundance of caution, thought it best that her husband not encourage the little man. Of course, the fisherman did what his wife asked, but it made him feel even guiltier than ever. But the monkey got his hundred thousand gold coins and things returned, more or less, to normal.

For the time being.

A few more years passed. The boy grew older and was eventually engaged to be married; Donlevy passed away and the fisherman's wife opened a second market stall at the edge of the other side of the forest selling shiny stones with artificial eyes glued onto them.

The fisherman's daughter-in-law-to-be was a beautiful young woman called Louella. One day she was visiting at the fisherman's home and sitting with her intended on an overturned herring crate, gazing into his eyes. The fisherman was watching proudly from the kitchen window as he scoured last night's pots and pans (he'd made mudskipper stew, which unfortunately had given his wife indigestion) when the merry tinkle of the front doorbell caught his ear.

Bowing low on the front stoop was the monkey.

With all his money, he had developed a taste for the finer things. His long and hairy fingers were now festooned with pearl-encrusted rings; he wore Persian slippers and a muffin cap of oriental silk;

and, most impressively, playing out from his neck with the sort of flamboyance that made Gottfried von Hohenlohe-Schillingsfürst of Vienna look like a brown onion, was a cape so long that the monkey's footmen had to gather it in for a full minute before the fisherman could close the door.

He waved away the fisherman's proffered hand as he pushed his way inside and made himself at home on the good chair by the fire.

'You know why I'm here, don't you?' said the monkey, looking about the room with a snooty expression on his face.

'Your wish?' sighed the fisherman.

'My SECOND wish,' said the monkey.

The fisherman sighed again and sat opposite the monkey on the second-best chair.

'I wish to be KING,' announced the monkey, without any further to-do, 'and rule this land from high atop Tancred Mountain.'

'From the castle?' asked the fisherman, blinking.

'Yes.'

'King?'

'That's right.'

'Ruling the land?'

'All I survey.'

'Well, um –'

'AND its people. They shall bow down before me and tremble at my sight.'

The fisherman had his head in his hands.

'What is it?' asked the monkey.

'Nothing, nothing,' muttered the fisherman.

'You seem upset,' observed the monkey, correctly.

'No, no,' said the fisherman, looking up with a weak smile. 'Um ... how long have I got to grant this wish, O Noble Monkey?'

'I wish it to be done instantaneously,' replied the monkey.

The fisherman nodded as if it might be possible and then pretended that a thought had occurred to him. 'You know,' he said, chancing some honesty, 'I might need a little extra time to arrange something like this.'

'You shall have TWENTY-FOUR HOURS,' proclaimed the monkey generously.

'I think I'm going to need *longer* than that,' said the fisherman. He'd broken into a sweat.

'All right then, twenty-FIVE.'

'A *week,* please! I'm going to need at least a week.'

The monkey stared off into the fire.

The fisherman was exceedingly worried. He didn't want the monkey to take away his beloved son, particularly on the eve of his wedding to Louella. Plus, the fisherman's wife was due home any moment and the last thing he wanted her to see was a monkey sitting on their best chair. Not because she didn't like monkeys; she loved all of God's creatures and would begrudge none a seat by the fire. It was just that the fisherman felt the sight would require some explanation – and this he was most keen to avoid. He looked down at his worn-out shoes for inspiration but found none. When he looked up again he was met with the monkey's yellow eyes boring into his very soul.

Suddenly the front door blew open and the fire snuffed out.

'You have your ONE WEEK,' said the monkey. Then he scampered out through the door, down the path and off into the bushes (as best he could with such an ungainly cape) just as the fisherman's wife happened through the gate, her arms full of loose sticks and rolls of ribbon to bundle them together.

'Was that a monkey I just saw, my love?' she asked her husband, who was standing guiltily on the porch.

'No, no,' he lied. 'How was work?'

And his wife proceeded to tell him at length. Apparently the shiny stones-with-eyes weren't selling that well.

✳

The very next day the fisherman went to Castle Tancred to see King Pangloss. He waited in line until nightfall, and was sent away.

He was only eventually allowed in because the recently knighted Royal Woodsman saw him crying in a ditch and took pity on him.

The Royal Woodsman knew the fisherman and his wife (he would sometimes buy her gaily coloured sticks for kindling). He offered to take the poor man inside through his personal entrance and contrive an introduction to the King, who he knew would be about to perform his ablutions in the Grand Bath Chamber, just off the Main Hall Vestibule and to the left.

And, sure enough, when they arrived, there was His Majesty hurrying up the steps, clutching his toiletries in a small chamois bag.

'Your Majesty!' exclaimed the Royal Woodsman to the surprise of the King, who was not expecting to run into anybody at this hour in his dressing-gown. 'Allow me to introduce the husband of the woman in the forest I buy your kindling from sometimes.'

The fisherman bowed low, unconsciously aping the monkey's flamboyance from the previous day.

'Oh, yes,' said the King vaguely in the direction of the fisherman, trying to be polite. He still owed a debt of gratitude to the Royal Woodsman for saving his daughter Mathilda and was often polite to him when their paths crossed. 'The young Princesses and I enjoy nothing more than reading the Bible together in the warmth of the East Library.'

'No, that's the kindling I get from the copse[2] at the back of the monastery, Your Majesty,' said the Royal Woodsman. 'I'm referring to the gaily coloured sticks we occasionally use to heat up your groom's kettle on Thursdays.'

'Of course, Sir Royal Woodsman,' said the King, pretending to remember and regarding the fisherman as if he were a new and interesting cake at a local fair. 'And how is your delightful wife?'

[2] A small bunch of trees; kind of like a clump.

'She is well, Your Majesty,' answered the fisherman, after a nod from the Royal Woodsman that it would be all right to respond. 'But I have a problem only soluble by the effervescent Imperial Wisdom of the Crown.'

King Pangloss liked being flattered and as he gave the impression of being interested in what he was being told, the fisherman explained it all: the monkey, the blond and blue-eyed son, the wishes, the week and the fact that he had not, as yet, told any of this to his wife.

The King stroked his impressive beard, which curled up at the end like a Persian slipper and sometimes, on special occasions, even had a bell on it. He was moved by the fisherman's plight but understandably reluctant to so readily give over his reign and kingdom to a monkey.

'If I do what you ask of me for the sake of your son, I will first have to check the legalities and protocol of all this with the Lord Chamberlain after my bath. Make a note of that, would you, Sir Royal Woodsman?' (The Royal

Woodsman, who had no pencil, did not.) 'But be warned: the passing of Royal Title to this lower-order primate will be for a LIMITED TIME ONLY.'

King Pangloss the Sanguine, for all his much vaunted no-nonsense iron goodwill and velvet fist, was a terribly pompous ass. Still, given that pointing this out would sometimes get your head lopped off and into a basket, it was best to keep your own counsel.

'Oh, yes, Your Majesty, of course,' blathered the fisherman. 'That is most generous and kind –'

'During which limited time you must renegotiate the terms of purchase for your foundling boy,' the King concluded with his eyes half-closed.

The fisherman could not have been happier (unless, of course, none of this had ever happened in the first place).

'Let this be a lesson to you,' said the King, loftily, 'of both my magnificence and the care you need to take when entering into contractual negotiations.'

The fisherman fell to the
King's feet and kissed them.
Fortunately for both men,
they had socks on them.

'The young Princesses and I are travelling to Byzantium for the summer anyway,' shrugged His Majesty. 'The castle will be vacant. Just be sure that the monkey is gone upon our return.'

The fisherman kissed the King's besocked feet some more and wept. The King, concerned that his bathwater might be getting cold, patted the fisherman on the head and left. The Royal Woodsman helped the still fawning fisherman up and ushered him from the castle, sending him on his way across the drawbridge with a wave and a wish to be remembered to his wife (with whom he occasionally shared a 'coffee').

The Royal Family left for their holidays as planned and the monkey was crowned by the puzzled Archbishop before a baffled audience of Nobles and Lords. The people, too, were rather confused by the whole thing but continued about their lives and very soon accepted as normal that they were being ruled by an animal. In fact, to be honest, it was an improvement.

The fisherman, though, found himself in a bit of a bind. Now that the monkey was King, it was very difficult to get to see him in order to renegotiate their arrangement. The fisherman would queue for days on end at the castle to no avail – and the Royal Woodsman couldn't help him anymore because, as part of the Royal Retinue, he had gone away on holiday as well. No, as time ticked unhelpfully by and the real monarch's return grew imminent, the fisherman worried more and more about the monkey finding out that he was

not really the King but only a Royal Pretender.

He and his son were out in the dam, hauling in the last of the summer trout (to be loaded on a wagon pulled by old Mr Bodkin from next door and bound for the town), when a splendid carriage drew up outside the house. A flurry of servants rolled out a carpet of pirate crimson and from the gilded interior of the coach, which verily glowed like the fabled Amber Room of Saint Petersburg (but with wheels), stepped the monkey.

The fisherman and his son knelt before him.

'Arise, fisherman,' said the monkey, doffing his crown and gloves and handing them to a lackey. 'I suppose you know why I'm here.'

The fisherman pretended he did not, in the vain hope that it would all go away.

'My THIRD wish.'

The vein on the fisherman's forehead began pulsing. The monkey was already King and the Master of All He Surveyed – what more could he possibly want?

'I want to be Emperor of the Universe and control all living creatures with my mind,' he proclaimed.

'You want to be ... a God?' stammered the fisherman.

The monkey paused a moment and then smiled. 'I want to be THE God. You have one week.'

And with that, the monkey scurried back into the carriage and, with a tumble of wheels, was gone. A cloud of dust could be seen over the rise in the road just as the fisherman's wife arrived home from work (a good day, too, in which she had shifted all her willow baskets and galvanised-iron hens).

'Was that the King?' she asked.

'No, no,' said her husband, making a face at such a notion. 'That was ... um, that was the ... er, Night Soil Collector.'

His wife laughed, thinking her husband was making a joke. 'The Night Soil Collector?' she repeated, squinting up at the sun. 'But it's three in the afternoon.'

'Yes,' said the fisherman, making elaborate hand gestures and smiling to cover his lying. 'The Night Soil Collecting business has been so brisk, you see, that they thought they'd do a *day shift* now as well.'

The fisherman's wife shook her head and kissed him on the cheek; and then, looping her arm in his, bustled inside telling him about her day.

The son said nothing.

The next day, the son asked if he could travel with his father on a trip he had planned to visit the local wizard. The fisherman had said he was visiting the wizard to sell him some carp. In truth, the fisherman hoped the wizard might be able to cast some sort of spell on the monkey to delude him into just THINKING he could control the universe, whereas really it would just go on as randomly as it always did. This wizard had already done such a Deluding Spell by accident last summer when Lamar the Cobbler came to see him for a baldness cure; Lamar's head still resembled a doorknob, but he was forever combing

it and asking people whether he should get his hair cut. Granted, it was a long shot as far as the monkey was concerned (the monkey was nowhere near as stupid as Lamar), but the fisherman was fast running out of options. The King was due home in TWO DAYS. Plus, he still hadn't mentioned any of this to his wife and the guilt was beginning to tell on him. All the fisherman's teeth had fallen out, he was losing his vision, and he had developed a limp (the local apothecary had told him he should get his leg removed, but his concerned wife said this would just make the limp worse).

And so the fisherman unburdened his troubles onto his son. He told him the whole story: the monkey, the deal, the first wish, the second wish and ... well, his son already knew the rest.

The young man said nothing at first. It was a lot for a simple fisherman's son to be told on a rough road to Wizard's Glen: that his parents were not his own and that he was one half of an unnatural bargain with a talking monkey. Good Lord, perhaps HE WASN'T EVEN HUMAN!

But he loved his father and so he put all that to one side and pondered how best to solve the dilemma.

'Father?' said the young man, after a while. 'I think I have a way out of our little problem.'

OUR little problem. At that moment, the fisherman could not have had any greater love for his son. He felt pride, too; his chest swelled so mightily he thought it might burst. He HAD been a good father all these years after all. Yes, the boy's mother was a fine woman, but she was at work a lot and would often arrive home late, after the boy had gone to bed. All she ever talked about was sticks and ribbons and how the bottom had fallen out of the googly-eyed stone market. No, the credit was all his for the fine and principled fellow that his son had grown into.

'I think we should kill the monkey,' said the young man.

The fisherman pulled back on the reins sharply and Mr Bodkin stuttered to a halt. The fisherman had never spoken a harsh word to his son in all their time together but on this occasion the fisherman scolded the boy for even having such a wicked thought. It was a sin, he told him, to kill any living creature, no matter how evil it was. For an hour they spoke as Mr Bodkin ate grass by the roadside: a loving father and an equally loving son, each putting their view to the other in a healthy exchange of views. In the end the fisherman turned around completely and agreed that the monkey had to go.

But what should be the method of dispatch?

The Wizard in the Glen – Balthazar the Magnificent – was said to possess a potion that could turn monkeys into easily-stepped-upon caterpillars. Unfortunately he was out of stock and fresh shipments were not due for a month. Balthazar, though, now fully apprised of the problem (the monkey, the child, the wishes, etc.) recommended the fisherman and his son visit Torino the Archer who, people said, could fire an arrow over a hundred miles directly into a sultana perched on the head of his idiot daughter, Carmella. So the fisherman and his boy travelled to meet Torino the Archer, and it turned out the claims were true. Unfortunately, it also turned out that was ALL Torino the Archer could do: hit a sultana off Carmella's head at a hundred miles. He couldn't hit *any other* target over *any other* distance – or even off *anyone else's* head. Torino, though, suggested they go and see Congee the Psychopath who led a band of marauders in the Dark Wood of Caliphy, just near the Voltonian Sulphur Lakes betwixt the Haunted Caves of Arkadian. For a handful of beads Congee and his men would vanquish one's enemies, no questions asked. Unfortunately, he 'didn't do monkeys'. It said so on his business card.

The fisherman and his son thanked the renowned psychopath for wasting their time and Congee, in return, chased them both through the swamp with his scythe.

On the long trip back home, dust on their faces and dried sweat over the body of Mr Bodkin, father and son sat in silence. Only the crush of earth under the big wooden wheels could be heard between the pleasing piping of spatchcock in the dale. But who was that sitting on a milestone on the outskirts of Wizard's Glen? Why, it was none other than Balthazar, his face rudely wrapped around a broad and gummy grin.

'I have found the solution to your problem, fisherman,' he announced, producing a small package of noisy crystals from somewhere in the folds of his gown.

Mr Bodkin reared up and whinnied and it took several worrying moments for both father and son to bring the horse under control.

'The crystals,' said Balthazar, as he shook them again (this time more quietly), 'when dissolved into a goblet of mead and gulped down, will produce a sleep of such deep and unshakable depth that the victim would, for all intents and purposes, be dead – but not actually dead.'

It was a practical solution that stepped neatly around any moral quandary about treading on a monkey after it was turned into a caterpillar. 'And the spell is strong, too,' added Balthazar. 'It can only be broken by the kiss of a handsome prince – and in my professional opinion no prince, regardless of their looks, is going to kiss a monkey. Especially an unconscious one.'

And so came the day – as days often do – when King

Pangloss was to return. The whole of the kingdom came out to greet him, which did rather confuse the monkey who, as we know, was under the impression that HE was King and already in residence. Needless to say, the monkey was furious.

As banners were being raised and standards hung, the monkey commanded his guards to arrest the fisherman and his son and fling them in the dankest dungeon of the castle. The King was less than an hour away when the jailor opened the door to their cell and the monkey stormed in.

'What is the meaning of this?' asked the monkey. 'Am I NOT King?'

The fisherman was too afraid to speak.

'Come on, man,' the monkey roared. 'Did you – or did you not – make me Ruler of this Kingdom with the power of life and death over its citizenry?'

'Well, yes –' began the fisherman.

'Were not coins struck with my face upon them? Was I not a just and fair Emperor whose reign was marked by wisdom and reason? Did I not just this week receive the

Regent of Saxony and his courtesan and treat them to lavish entertainments? Am I not known throughout the civilised world as one of Europe's Most Wonderful Monarchs?'

'Of course, Your Majest–'

'Then why did my Stool Groom just refer to me as "Mr Peanuts"?'

The fisherman had no answer. His son bided his time, seemingly preoccupied with the chain of a manacle fixed to the wall. But he was thinking, for he was a very WISE young man.

'Your mute insolence is answer enough,' said the monkey, and he turned to the jailor. 'Fetch me the Executioner. My last official act as King will be to separate the heads of these two treacherous worms from their worthless bodies.'

'But Your Majesty,' said the fisherman's son as the monkey was about to leave. 'You have asked my father to make you a God, have you not?'

'THE God,' said the monkey.

'Then it follows, at some point, that you must cease

to be a mortal King, in order to ascend to the next realm.'

That made sense. 'Go on.'

'Well, might it not stand to reason,' the son went on, 'that only upon the former King reclaiming his throne will Your Majesty then become the Supreme Being and Creator of the Universe?'

'That's exactly right,' said the fisherman, smiling at his son for his cleverness but not really adding much.

The monkey beamed, his past mood forgotten. 'YES!' he said, clapping his paws together as if he were one of those wind-up monkeys with a pair of cymbals. 'Come – let us adjourn to the Grand Ballroom for the ceremony.'

＊

The Grand Ballroom was bedecked with colours and candles and was filled with everyone who was anyone, and a great many others who weren't: Archbishops and Mothers Superior and Abbots and Nuns and Deans and Chancellors and Dukes and Duchesses and Counts and Barons and Knights and Dames and Thanes and Scribes and Reeves and Ladies-in-Waiting and Musketeers and Yeoman as well as lowly Butlers and Cup-Bearers and Falconers and Ushers and Serving Girls and Heralds and Squires and Wenches and Pedlars and Minstrels and Keepers of the Seal and even the seals themselves. Entertainment was provided by the Court Jester, Doc, who played the miniature crumhorn like an angel (his career had blossomed since leaving that all-dwarf septet). The only person not there was the Stool Groom, whom the monkey had earlier ordered be encased in a mask and banished to the isle of Sainte-Marguerite. This caused a lot of problems later on when people wanted to go to the toilet and no-one was there to give directions.

The King was very happy to be home. The holiday hadn't gone well; Byzantium had been overrun by plague-carrying infidels and he and his daughters had been forced to share a castle with some Ostrogoths as the one they had booked had been sacked. Mathilda had gone to a dance with Theodoric the Great and come home with a tattoo.

It was a disaster.

The monkey graciously returned his crown to the bemused King and there was much cheering and carousing into the night.

Balthazar the Wizard turned up drunk and fell in the fountain, dissolving the crystals he had secreted on his person (to nil effect); Torino the Archer was called upon to display his formidable skills but, also being drunk, missed the sultana on his idiot daughter's head and instead fired the arrow out of the palace oculus, where it travelled a hundred miles to the property next door to the fisherman's and split the corn-cob pipe Mr Bodkin was smoking; Congee the Psychopath and his band of marauders, who weren't invited but turned up anyway, treated the assembled throng to a re-enactment of the Massacre at Ayyadieh. The fisherman and his son used this last distraction to try to sneak out, but the monkey saw what was going on and swung across the room on several chandeliers, dropping down neatly by the doors to block their exit.

'And where do you think you are going?' he asked, narrowing his yellow eyes and baring his even yellower teeth.

'Us?' said the fisherman, pointing to himself and his son. 'Why, we were just ... er ... we thought – I mean, it's such a lovely evening we thought we'd – that is to say –'

'Spare me your hemming and hawing,' the monkey spat, 'and tell me why no-one is paying any attention to me.' With a grand sweep of his arm he indicated the crowd enjoying themselves and, seemingly, indifferent to his presence.

'Well, there's a lot going on,' said the fisherman, laughing nervously. 'Balthazar falling in the fountain, the archery display, Congee, Little Doc's wailing crumhorn during "Fowles in the Frith" –'

'But I am GOD!' exclaimed the monkey. 'And I think I deserve a little more attention than a bunch of empty diversions.'

'These are secular times, O Lord,' volunteered the fisherman's son.

'He's right,' concurred the fisherman. 'Church attendances are way down.'

The monkey had to concede that this was true. Even

the Venerable Bead had difficulty drawing a crowd these days. Still ... he *was* God.

'I am an omniscient and supernatural being, am I not?'

'Well, yes –'

'I can transcend time and space, can I not?'

'Of course –'

'Then why can't I also compel mankind to worship me and do my bidding?' The monkey turned to a group of people ignoring him and concentrated hard.

Nothing.

'Well?' said the monkey, turning back to the fisherman and his son, the backs of his wrists upturned on his hips.

'Mankind has free will, you see,' explained the fisherman's son.

'What?'

'A gift from you, in your infinite wisdom,' he added.

The monkey was flattered by the idea of his own cosmic benevolence. 'Yes, I suppose it *was* extraordinarily generous of me,' he admitted.

'You are a just and fair God, O Monkey,' said the son. 'You know – being all-knowing – that the path to man's salvation can be only one he CHOOSES to take. You rightly see – being all-seeing – that man's redemption is only something that can be earnt by personal sacrifice and that one cannot have personal sacrifice if that something being sacrificed is TAKEN rather than GIVEN.'

The monkey nodded, put his arms around the fisherman and his son and walked to an open casement window, which he gazed out of self-consciously.

The fisherman offered him a bowl of mead, which he took. 'You speak the truth,' the monkey concluded after a sip. 'It's all part of the meaning of life, isn't it? This business of intermingling God's will with the free will of humanity.'

The fisherman and his son were eyeing that open window.

The monkey, resigned to being something of a non-interventionist God, bid his guests goodbye and returned to wandering around the Grand Ballroom eating canapés and making small talk with people who politely concealed their irritation. It was something the Duke of Kent refined to an art many hundreds of years later.

The fisherman and his son, meanwhile, returned home just in time to greet the fisherman's wife, who was a little late as she was exhausted from a busy day at her stalls and had met up with the Royal Woodsman for a much-needed coffee. She had some good news, too: she was pregnant.

The fisherman was overjoyed that he would be a father again and his son couldn't wait to become a big brother. If it was a boy, agreed his parents, he was to be called Pangloss in gratitude to the King; if it was a girl, she would be called Mathilda in honour of His Majesty's daughter.

If it was a dwarf, promised the fisherman to himself, he would call the child Donlevy. He would tell his wife about the promise one day – for if he had learnt anything at all from his adventure, it was to never promise anything you couldn't deliver on.

In the end it was triplets (one of each) and the fisherman's wife decided to name them all after the Royal Woodsman.

The Magic Beans

and the PEDLAR'S

WIFE

and the Cow

When Tom Thumb returned home after the war it was in triumph. He had fought the Turk as valiantly and courageously as could any man who stood no bigger than a thumb, and he had accomplished much else besides: maidens saved, relics reclaimed, heathen temples pillaged – plus a few surprises, too. Yes, there were quite a few feathers in his tricorn hat, but the most splendid of all in the plume – and the deed for which he had been promoted to no less a rank than General – was his single-handed rescuing of all of Hamelin's rats from inside a mountain.

Had he done this in the kingdom of King Pangloss the Sanguine, he would have been set upon a pillory[3] and had fruit thrown at him (for, as you know, rats were not liked at all) but in Hamelin, they were fond of their rodents and the rat was highly prized. No sign of Hamelin's missing children, though, which was a pity because the people of Hamelin, as much as they liked rats, LOVED their children.

His services to ratdom aside, the King was nevertheless impressed with General Thumb's celebrity and so had Sheriff Belknap proclaim that Tancred Town's native son have the Freedom of the City. And, to the cheers of the citizenry, he

[3] Kind of like a merry-go-round but without horses (and you get tied to it with ropes).

was awarded a generous pension and the title to a neat-as-a-pin cottage all the way on the other side of the forest, just across the River Weser.

One day soon after, while gathering figs in the forest to make jam, the General met and fell in love with the now grown up (older but no taller) and bespectacled Tiny Poncho Girl, who was en route through the woods to visit her wicked step-grandfather, Ardamanic of Scatera. After a whirlwind courtship, she and Tom were married with great ceremony at Tancred Cathedral by the Pope himself, who happened to be visiting on holiday.

Their union was blessed
with such issue as befits the
love between a dwarf and a
faerie: an extraordinarily
minuscule boy, smaller
than even a thumb, whom
they called Jacques.

Jacques, being infinitesimal, was considerably shorter than even his mother and father (which made him very short indeed – about the size of a pinkie toe), but what he lacked in stature he more than made up for in ambition. No scheme was too outlandish for Jacques; no prize beyond his reach; no goal which, in his estimation, he could not achieve with ease.

Only his incompetence at almost everything he turned his hand to undid him. Business after business failed lamentably: water-carrier, wagon-mender, stonecutter, candle-maker, thatch-gatherer – it didn't matter what the trade, Jacques proved a master at none. Eventually, his ill-founded faith in himself gave way to a ruthless cunning to get what he wanted in life and, sadly, he became a man not to be trusted. When his father died in a fig-gathering mishap that no-one thought anything of at the time, Jacques ploughed his mother's inheritance into opening a tailor's shop.

Now, Jacques no more knew how to stitch a seam than he knew how to abseil a hedgehog and within only a few weeks the business was bankrupt and the bailiff had seized his mother's neat-as-a-pin cottage. So that they might eat, Jacques had to sell off the only remaining thing he and his mother owned: a beautiful white cow by the name of Ethel.

To market, to market went Jacques and Ethel – and on the way, they met an old pedlar whose name escapes me. Jacques didn't care who he was either; to him the guy was simply a mark/a rube/a greenhorn/a sucker/a sap. Jacques conned the poor fellow out of the entire bag of magic beans he had with him and, waving a merry goodbye to a befuddled Ethel, Jacques hurried home to show his mother how clever he was.

Jacques' mother may well have been proud of her boy (for she loved him dearly despite his many faults). But the old pedlar's wife was furious when all her husband brought back from the market was an old cow. Yes, it was a very attractive white cow with a lovely name but it was not, she felt, the profitable end of the bargain.

'Those beans were worth millions,' she cried. 'You could have traded them for a farm, or a gold mine. Why, this cow is so old it probably doesn't even give milk anymore.'

It was true, admitted the old pedlar. Jacques had explained that the reason he was taking the cow to market was that it had stopped giving milk. Jacques had, in fact, been very honest about that (knowing that the best lies are those larded with truth). The old pedlar tried to tell his wife that Jacques and his mother had been very upset at having to sell their cow (who was more of a friend, really) but because they were very poor they really had no choice. The old man had felt sorry for Jacques, you see.

'Then you're a bigger fool than you look,' snapped his wife. 'Fancy a pedlar of your age and experience falling for an old sob story like that. How long have you been in the peddling game?'

The old pedlar tried to remember (he wasn't very good at arithmetic) but his wife wasn't really interested in hearing an answer. She just wanted to tell him what a good-for-nothing he was. 'Why, I could have taken those beans to the market and come back with ten thousand cows!' she told him.

As good as he wasn't at maths, the old pedlar couldn't see how she could possibly have bought TEN THOUSAND cows. She'd only given him a handful of beans — seven or eight at most, perhaps four. Plus, Jacques had seemed like a decent fellow. He'd wept when he'd said that he and his mother were starving and the old pedlar had thought they would enjoy eating the beans, which, if portioned out carefully, could last one or two meals (although the second meal might have to not involve any beans) ...

'But they were MAGIC beans, you silly man,' his wife interrupted. 'Balthazar the Wizard said he'd never seen anything like them in all his one-hundred-and-twenty years when he sold them to me. He said they were ENORMOUSLY powerful and capable of ANYTHING.'

These beans sounded dangerous, thought the old pedlar. He was suddenly worried for Jacques and his poor mother.

What if they exploded as they ate them?

Or turned into weasels?

Or turned THEM

into weasels?

He said nothing more, though,
for fear it would incur the further
crossness of his wife.

'Now get that cow out of here and into the barn,' his wife continued. 'And while you're at it, you can move your own things in there as well.'

The old pedlar, crestfallen and sad and another word that meant the same thing, led Ethel from the house – first collecting his bedding and toiletries from upstairs – and adjourned to the ramshackle barn for the night. As he patted Ethel and fed her an oat or two (or fourteen), the old man cursed his own twittishness and fell into a fitful sleep.

✳

The next day, Jacques – whose mother had hurled the
magic beans out of the window in exasperation
the previous evening (making sure
Jacques didn't see, for she loved him
dearly and would never want to
hurt his feelings) – awoke from
his equally uncomfortable
slumber on his threadbare
gunny-sack to find several
huge, gnarled beanstalks
growing from the back
garden of the shanty
they were squatting in
– just across the road
from their old neat-as-
a-pin cottage – all the
way up into the clouds.

He climbed one of the beanstalks as far as he could go to a giant manor house on the precipice of a mountain, broke in, stole some bags of silver and, once he clambered all the way back down again, used the silver as collateral to negotiate a new lease on a new tailor's shop.

Of course, Jacques was no better a tailor this time around than he had been a few weeks before. He, like you and I, didn't know a *houppelande* from a *jopula* and so, this time, sensibly hired some goblins to run the business instead. Now, the trouble with goblins is that while their work is impeccable, they are VERY greedy and so what was left of Jacques' stolen silver after he paid the rent did not last very long. Soon enough he needed to shinny back up the beanstalk and through the clouds to the giant manor house

again in order to steal
something else of value. This
time, a gold-egg-laying goose.
The goblins were happy to accept
a gold egg per day in return for
the excellent management of Jacques'
tailoring shop – and run it excellently they
did. Customers were happy, the landlord was
happy, Jacques and his mother were able to
buy back their old neat-as-a-pin cottage
and, while it was being repainted at great
expense, they both got to go on a luxury
holiday to Foulness Island, where
they had the time of their lives.

'More fun than when I was
invited to Hamelin to unveil a
statue of my late husband,' wrote the
former Tiny Poncho Girl in the visitors'
book at the Maplin Screw Pile
Lighthouse where they stayed.

So happy was Jacques that in a fit of unusual-for-him generosity, he donated some of his unearnt wealth to Hamelin so the civic fathers could erect an additional statue of himself to stand alongside his father (life-size, so it didn't actually cost that much).

Not that any of this was at all about money, of course. No, no, no – most of it was about myth-making. You see, while the goblins beavered away at night in secret, making surcoats and doublets for the fine gentlemen of the city, Jacques' reputation as a master tailor took root and spread throughout the land so virulently that very soon even Jacques himself came to believe it. So full of his own legend was he that he had the goblins embroider a special girdle for him to wear that bore the words 'Several in One Blow', a blatant lie he often told about the number of buttons he could simultaneously sew onto a wedding tunic. The boast did lose something when reduced to abbreviated needlepoint, but nevertheless, Jacques took to the streets in it almost every day – a monstrous display of hubris unseen since the King's favourite Lancer, Tybalt the Vain, went into battle against an erupting volcano armed with only a cottonbud.

The villagers could not help but be impressed by Jacques' braggadocio, even if they didn't know exactly what 'Several in One Blow' meant and assumed it had something to do with the slaying of giants. Word of this supposed great deed eventually reached Tancred where the Prince Regent, Hubert (ruling in lieu of his uncle, King Pangloss, who had taken to his bed with St Vitus Dance), sent word that the brave young tailor from the forest he'd been hearing so much about should attend him at once at the palace, so that he might have a champion less like charcoal than Tybalt the Vain. Also, the Prince needed an emergency set of coronation robes to wear should his poor uncle succumb – and who better to whip up something splendid than the master tailor simply everybody in the kingdom was raving about?

'I wish the most wavishing fabwics to be wapped about me,' demanded Prince Hubert, a fey little man with spots. 'A wange of gawments never before seen by anyone in the human wace.'

It was quite the task the Prince had set before him, but Jacques bowed and swept his feathered beret grandly in a sudden clockwise arc that had the Royal Guards half-grabbing at the hilts of their swords. 'Your Magnificent Highness shall have a set of clothing not only unseen before in the history of Man, but the likes of which will never be seen again,' promised the so-called 'tailor'.

Hubert clapped his hands and jumped up and down like a yappy chihuahua keen on a piece of sausage. He was something of a fashion plate and his wardrobe was full of golden-fleece wimples, gryphon-feather mitres and thigh boots made of baby sable.

Jacques was sequestered in a gilded room with servants to wait on him, food piled high to the ceiling and a plush bed with a feather mattress so soft it was like sleeping on frangipane. At the very centre of the room was a beautiful mahogany spinning wheel 'liberated' from a Venetian convent during a recent crusade. The Prince had seen the Royal Physician (a former barber from Smyrna) shaking his head gravely when last checking on the King's humours and so gave Jacques only two weeks to create his creation: a creation of such breathtaking and original majesty that the milk of human kindness in the bosom of God in Heaven would curdle with jealousy.

The trouble was, of course, that Jacques was hopeless. Not only could he not think of anything special enough to make, but he couldn't make it even if he could. He sent a message to the goblins to come and help him but they refused unless he upped their already extortionate fee.

Jacques was forced to sneak out of the castle under the cover of darkness, scale the beanstalk again, break into the manor house beyond the clouds and steal something else of enormous value.

Unfortunately all he could find without the lights on was a self-playing lyre that the goblins weren't at all interested in. 'What the hell are we supposed to do with that?' asked the Head Goblin very rudely.

So Jacques had to come up with something all by himself.

Day after day, night after night, Jacques racked his brain for some sort of idea. None was forthcoming. Often, when he felt he might have been on the cusp of inspiration, it escaped him before he could seize on it, like scrabbling at a morning shadow at sunrise or a greased eel as it disappeared down a fish gutter's sluice pipe.

The other thing that made it difficult was the Prince Regent himself. Hubert was constantly bothering Jacques with orders to go and vanquish the giants who he imagined were threatening his kingdom. Giants? The only giants Jacques knew were Mr and Mrs Ostermann, who owned the manor house he had been robbing up in the clouds. And they were only giants in a relative sense, in that they were a tallish couple compared with Jacques – but then, so was mostly everyone. There was a moral dimension to Jacques' difficulty as well. The little fellow had done a lot of bad things in his time, but he'd never vanquished anybody. Yet Prince Hubert was insistent.

'There is a weason for this wegal wequest,' he confided to Jacques after shutting the door to his sewing room. 'I wish to impwess the Pwincess so she may agwee to mawwy me.'

'Princess Mathilda?' asked Jacques, who rather liked her himself. She was now all grown up and, despite the tattoo, still as beautiful as she always had been.

'The vewy one,' said Hubert with a secret smile. 'How could any woman wesist a man who bwings her such a wemawkable pwize. Even if it is ...' (and here he leant into Jacques, tapped the side of his nose and whispered) '... *by pwoxy.*'

'But Your Highness,' asked Jacques, a little troubled. 'Isn't Princess Mathilda your cousin?'

'Yes. And what of it?'

'But surely marrying your cousin is –'

'Woyalty has been interbweeding for centuwies,' snapped Hubert, his voice pinched with adenoidal huff. 'It is how we maintain our pedigwee.'

'Won't your children risk being chinless and bald haemophiliacs?'

The Prince Regent reared up, his nostrils flaring. 'Who am I to bweak with a twadition going back centuwies? Now be off with you, young Jacques, and bwing me back the lawgest and most tewwifing giant in all the land.'

And with that, he turned on his Georgian heels and tottered from the room, not even pausing when he lost his wig on a chandelier.

Again, Jacques ascended the beanstalk – this time armed with a sword – climbing beyond the clouds, over the fence and into the mountain home of the 'giant' Ostermanns. He vanquished them easily (they were asleep) and on his way out he stole a pair of Mercury Swift dancing boots and a Cloak of Invisibility. Maybe they would fetch a couple of dollars.

※

While all this had been going on, the old pedlar and Ethel had visited Gustav the Lawyer, who had an office between two butchers' shops in Shambles Lane. The place reeked horribly but Gustav knew the law like the back of his hand – which was where he wrote most of it down. 'Easier to consult during a trial,' he explained.

The pedlar wanted justice, and at a reasonable price. He wanted to sue Jacques for fraud. He wanted all the riches that Jacques had accrued since swindling him out of his beans: the silver, the goose, the refurbished neat-as-a-pin cottage, the goblin-operated tailor's business, the job at the castle, even the self-playing lyre. Gustav listened for almost the full five minutes of the 'first free consultation' before he held up his hand, rose unsteadily from his desk, splashed out a tankard of absinthe (it was, after all, eleven in the morning) and gulped it down as a starving bear would a swan.

'In exchange for Ethel,' Gustav announced as he poured himself another drink, 'I am prepared to represent you, sir, in legal proceedings against this Jacques person. Moreover, I am prepared, sir, to take the case all the way to a first hearing if necessary.' He slammed down his tankard on the old chocked-up door he was using as a desk with

the theatrical flair that made him the darling of the Petty Claims jurisdiction, before adding with an involuntary wink, 'Hopefully, sir, there will be a settlement well before that, of which I would be entitled to forty per cent in commission plus various fees and expenses.'

The last two items were delivered in a parenthesis of inaudible mumbling and an indistinct fluttering of fingers. The two men agreed and as Gustav toasted the arrangement with a bottle or two more of absinthe, the old pedlar spent the rest of the afternoon signing over his house and whatever else he owned.

The old pedlar's wife was sitting with her sister on the weather-beaten porch of her hovel. They were talking about their husbands.

'Well, mine has his moments,' laughed the old pedlar wife's sister, who was married to the fisherman from the previous tale. 'Mine almost ruined us once by granting three wishes to a monkey.'

'They're all the same,' sighed the
pedlar's wife, shaking her head.
'Nothing between their
ears but horse hair
and helium.'

   The two women
laughed and sipped their Bovril as
over the hill, off in the distance, the
old pedlar trudged towards them.
His wife could see he was cow-less.

'Look at him,' she said with a snort. 'I sent him off to take the cow for a walk this morning and he's completely forgotten her. Probably still tethered outside the local pub.'

'If it's not drink or monkeys, it's princesses,' said her sister, not unkindly. 'That young miller's wife down the road was telling me she caught her husband kissing one in a glass coffin outside that dwarves' place near Kestler's Mill.'

'Dead?'

'Dead*ish*.'

'Disgusting.'

'She said he said he was captivated by her beauty. Divorced now, of course.'

'You can't trust 'em.'

The fisherman's wife DID trust her husband. He'd only ever lied to her once and, while it was a considerable lie involving a magic monkey and the theft of thousands of silver coins and the duping of the entire kingdom, she had forgiven him and she loved him. But she also loved her sister and knew there wasn't much point disagreeing with her when she was ranting.

'That sort of thing is for the ruling classes,' the old pedlar's wife continued. 'I caught mine trying to rescue a princess from a dragon once. I said to him, "You leave her there, chained to that rock, where she belongs." Silver hands, you know.'

'Really?'

'Yes, well, they're the ones you've got to watch out for.'

The old pedlar, still a way off, gave his wife a cheery wave. She ignored him.

'Mind you, I wouldn't complain if one of these high-born types came and rescued me,' she said with a sly smile. 'Nearly happened to me last February.'

'Never.'

Her sister nudged her. 'As God is my witness.' She drew a cross on her heart with her finger and leant in, keen to tell the story before her husband arrived at the gatepost. 'I was washing some rags,' she whispered. 'You know, winter was coming and I wanted to make sure they were dried before the house flooded –'

'Yes, yes –'

'Anyway, I was doing a flick and fold and I hear the bell go on the door and so I look up and who walks in but one of those von Fürstenberg princes –'

'Egon or Nepomuck?'

'Egon, I think. Anyway he's got this glass slipper, right? And he says to me, "Is this yours? For if it be, I shall marry thee."'

'Nice rhyme,' the fisherman's wife giggled. She did like rhymes.

'I know. I mean, how could I resist?'

'Well, what did you say?'

'Well, before I can say anything, he's got me on the couch with my leg up, trying to slide it on. Of course, it don't fit too well, what with my bunions and that spur I've got on the back of my heel, but it was nice to have been in the running, you know –'

'Great story.'

'I tell you, I've never felt so alive.'

'Who'd he end up marrying in the end?' The fisherman's wife loved happy endings.

'Some chimney sweep from the town. Broken home. Stepmother's got two daughters, neither of whom are oil paintings –'

The face of the old pedlar's wife suddenly hardened into a hatchet the moment her once-fetching-viridian-green-but-now-more-the-colour-of-a-dead-praying-mantis eyes fell upon what her husband was carrying up the garden path: a hefty armful of legal documents tied up with magenta ribbon.

'What have you gone and done now, you silly man?' she cried.

'All our problems are over, my petal,' said the pedlar proudly, 'for I have secured the services of Gustav the Lawyer.'

The pedlar's wife let out a wail that shook the trees of their birds. She slapped the papers from his hands.

'A *lawyer?!!*' she yelled as he scurried to collect the pages about her feet. 'It's not enough that you've been fleeced by that little upstart tailor, no. You want to be cheated out of what little we have left by a lawyer?!!'

'But –'

But the pedlar's wife was in no mood for buts and stormed off over the hill to sort out this matter herself, once and for all, with her sister following close behind trying to calm her down.

First, she stopped by the Royal Woodsman's house to borrow his axe – her sister had told her about him (and he was every bit as handsome and strong and rugged as she'd said). He asked them both in for a coffee as Gretel and Hansel were off on an orienteering course and wouldn't be home 'til dark (if at all). The two women agreed, just to be polite, but after several cups and too many oatcakes they reminded him about the axe and he took them to his little shed in the Enchanted Glade to show them his collection. It was impressive.

'I've got everything here,' he said proudly, as he opened the door and let the light stream in. 'What do you need it for? Splitting, felling, or hewing? I've got broad axes, hand axes, throwing axes, battle axes, climbing axes, ice axes, pickaxes, pollaxes, hatchets, tomahawks –'

Through the floating motes of dust could be seen every type of axe imaginable, all glinting, clean, greased and freshly stone-sharpened. In pride of place – at the very centre of the array and surrounded by dozens of candles – was the gleaming stave-handled axe with the bearded Frankish head that the Royal Woodsman had famously used to rescue Grandma all those pages ago. The axe that had earnt him his title and lands and reputation and honour. Above it was a sign that said: 'My First and Most Beloved Axe. Retired After Twenty Years of Faithful Service. NOT TO BE USED UNDER ANY CIRCUMSTANCES.'

'That's the one,' said the pedlar's wife, pointing. And she tore it from the wall.

To the shanty across the road from Jacques' mother's old neat-as-a-pin cottage they all went, to cut down the beanstalk. Jacques' mother didn't mind at all as she was sick of it and wanted to plant some rhubarb instead. No-one thought to tell her that Jacques was still up there – but then, no-one knew except the Prince Regent (and he had

forgotten
anyway).

Jacques
– who was at
the very top of the
beanstalk struggling with
his bloodied sword, the Cloak of
Invisibility and the pair of Mercury
Swift dancing boots – had to hold on fast as
the vibrations from the frenzied chopping down below
almost shook him loose. He tried to put on the Mercury
Swift dancing boots so that he might scramble down the
beanstalk with superhuman speed but unfortunately they
were far too big for him (even when he tried to put them on
over his own shoes) and they slipped off.

FLOOMPH!!

FLOOMPH!!

The Mercury Swift dancing boots landed at the foot
of the stalk, narrowly missing the old pedlar's wife as she

readied the axe one last time. Onlookers had gathered
from nearby houses to watch, and Jacques' mother was
kindly serving them biscuits while they enjoyed the
entertainment. She always served biscuits when
her old friend, the Royal Woodsman,
came to visit. Everyone took
two each or maybe three,

but the fisherman's wife took far more than was polite and hid them in her skirts for later sale at her shop. Several pixies gnawed at a single biscuit from atop a toadstool. With such a crowd around her, though, the pedlar's wife got nervous and her swing was wildly way off. She completely missed the V-cut prepared for her by the Royal Woodsman so the stalk would fall the right way.

A dreadful crack echoed through the forest, scattering birds and lovers, and the giant legume began to fall north instead of south, its tilting trunk first crushing to bits Jacques' neat-as-a-pin cottage across the road. Its mighty stalk followed after, and with increasing velocity fell across the forest in a direct line towards Castle Tancred, wreaking a hundred miles of havoc on the way.

Why, it split in two the Chicken Little Observatory on Dunphy Hill and sent a rockslide over Donlevy's Cave. It shattered utterly the dreaded Dark Wood of Caliphy, tore asunder the bridge over the Voltonian Sulphur Lakes, sealed forever the Haunted Caves of Arkadian with atomised scree, pulverised the practice tree of Torino the Archer and only narrowly missed Balthazar the Wizard, who just managed to outrun it by escaping across the glen on old Mr Bodkin.

Balthazar's cries of 'The beanstalk is falling! The beanstalk is falling!' as he galloped through hamlet and village did little to raise an alarm, because unless you know it's a GIANT beanstalk that's falling it doesn't sound that serious. It was only after the beanstalk had crashed through their homes and businesses that people realised how helpful the warning *might* have been had it been properly phrased. Hengest and Hors, for example, had just finished constructing an architectural tour de force: an elaborate shoe-shaped bungalow for the aged mother of Lamar the Cobbler. She and the many orphaned children she looked after were just about to move in when the beanstalk flattened the entire structure down to its very sole. Of course, Peatbog McGinty – who happened to be across the road renovating Rumplestilt-something's barn – couldn't wait to run and tell the two brothers of their misfortune, but before he could even down his hammer, the tumbling plant tore through the roof he was working on, cleaving the entire building in two and destroying his billy-wagon.

On and on the beanstalk fell, splintering everything in its path: Shambles Lane, Hovels Row, the Maplin Screw Pile Lighthouse, Scrapefoot's Bog, even the little house of the Boy Who Cried Wolf (who still wasn't home). All gone. When news of the ongoing destruction reached Sheriff Belknap, he put down his rubber stamp and pushed back from his desk, a look of concern crawling over his features. There was, he mused, little point approving the Heritage Listing of Baba the Cannibal's lovingly restored Candy Slaughterhouse if it was very shortly no longer going to exist.

'How long do we have?' he asked the out-of-breath knave at his door.

'Less than twelve seconds,' was the reply.

Belknap turned to his window, raising a spyglass to his one good eye. A plume of dust and debris was rolling through the forest towards them, sucking in treetops as the toppling beanstalk sliced through the clouds and blacked out the main street to Tancred in a rapidly lengthening shadow.

'Then there is no time to lose,' he said, a little too slowly. 'Get me the Royal Woodsman.'

The Royal Woodsman was, however, uncontactable. Seeing his beloved forest under threat, he had donned the Mercury Swift dancing boots dropped by Jacques in an earlier paragraph and was presently racing, with gathering speed, alongside the collapsing stalk, following its trajectory towards the castle.

The Prince Regent, meanwhile, oblivious to the impending annihilation of his impending kingdom, was in his parlour leafing through swatches of fabric with his friend and fellow fashion plate, Gottfried von Hohenlohe-Schillingsfürst of Vienna. Hubert wished to re-cover all of the palace couches, as he was sick to death of his uncle's clan tartan. He and Gottfried shrieked with delight as they flipped over ever-more audacious patterns and failed to hear the sounds of their approaching doom.

Even more meanwhile, the lovely and still beautiful and now-of-marriageable-age Mathilda was in the forest with her best friend, the curly blonde-haired girl, kissing salamanders on the banks of Lake Nimue. You see, they had run out of frogs and the curly blonde-haired girl had suggested they move on to lizards instead. Mathilda, though, was quite firm about confining their advances to amphibians.

'But I don't trust them, Matty,' argued the blonde girl. 'I read somewhere that salamanders sometimes burst into flames.'

'Pish,' said the Princess in rebuttal. It was more sweet than rude.

'I'm telling you, they're dangerous. I'm not having my hair burnt off again.' (A year ago, the curly blonde-haired girl's beautiful golden locks had been consumed by flames when she had mistakenly kissed a baby dragon.)

'Wicked witches DO NOT turn handsome princes into lizards,' said Mathilda, pecking a promising-looking newt on the cheek. 'They're just TOO ugly.' The newt remained a newt despite her kiss and so the Princess tossed it back into the water.

'At least let me kiss a toad,' begged Blondie.

'Absolutely not,' said Mathilda, who had grown into a resolute woman with a strong will (two very attractive qualities). 'Toads are EVEN UGLIER than lizards!'

She was right, of course – and it was never wise to argue with a Princess even if she wasn't. Blondie sighed and scooped up an axolotl – but as she did so, she spied out of the corner of her eye, in a small rowboat under a tree, a sleeping monkey. At least it was a mammal, she thought. She released the axolotl and hurried over, careful not to be seen by the Princess (who was busy wiping some pond scum off her next conquest) but just as Blondie bent down to kiss the snoring creature on the lips, the sun was suddenly blotted out and there came a tremendous roar as the top-most crown of the beanstalk rained down towards them.

Both women, saucer-eyed and frozen with fear, would most surely have been driven into the ground like tent pegs had they not been plucked up and spirited out of harm's way just in time by the fleet-footed blur that was the Royal Woodsman.

On his back they clung as he outran the tip-top bit of the falling stalk, which ended its toppling by taking out the eastern drum tower of Castle Tancred, including (unfortunately) the turret in which the now late King Pangloss had been trying to get some sleep.

Jacques too, still clinging on for dear life to the uppermost leaf on the tip-top bit of the very crown of the beanstalk, did not survive. No-one knew what happened to the monkey.

When the Prince Regent later inspected the disaster area, all he deemed worthy of salvage was the Cloak of Invisibility, which he mistakenly thought Jacques had made for him in the event of his coronation.

He wore it proudly the very next day in a splendid pageant worthy of a newly crowned boyish King. Of course the cloak, being itself invisible (for it was a very SPECIAL Cloak of Invisibility that didn't quite work properly), meant that the crowds gathered along the roadside as Hubert tottered past could see right through it to his pale, skinny, naked, spotty body. No-one knew quite where to look but it would have been almost High Treason to turn away, so they didn't – and only one of the King's thousands of subjects dared yell out the obvious: the Boy Who Cried Wolf (it was his day off). His cry of 'Hey, nudie!' caught on and by the time young King Hubert arrived back at the palace, the people as one were chanting it over and over and His Majesty was blushing so much that everyone thought he had rubella. He was sent to his bed by the Royal Physician with a pot of salve and a prayer book. Needless to say, he never won over and married Princess Mathilda. Instead, she ruled the kingdom herself and did a fine job of it, too.

One of her first proclamations was to order the gathering up of all the giant beans from the felled stalk as they were sufficient to feed the subjects of her blight-benighted kingdom for a full year. Twelve months of an exclusive all-bean diet for everyone was also very good for the sales of potpourri, so the fisherman's wife made a fortune.

In fact, they all lived happily ever after all.

Ending
the
END

There was once a butterfly. As he was storing nuts for the winter in a tree, a duck walked past and laughed at him.

'Why do you waste your days worrying about the future?' said the duck. 'Life is for living.'

The butterfly was furious and fluttered off after the duck as it waddled down to the pond to go floating. 'Living in the moment is fine when you're young,' the butterfly yelled, 'but you'll soon discover that with maturity comes a sense of responsibility for tomorrow.'

The duck threw a stone at the butterfly to scare him away, but it struck him on the head instead and killed him.

The duck was mortified at what he'd done, and buried the butterfly in the rose garden of an ogre.

The next season, the first of the ogre's roses to bloom looked just like a butterfly, and the ogre fell in love with it. He would spend every day in the garden, talking to it and playing it songs on his lute; once, he even rather misguidedly brought it flowers.

The ogre's wife grew jealous of the butterfly rose and one day, while the ogre went to the village on important business (buying a washing machine), the wife plucked the rose and hurled it into the river.

The river took the rose all the way to the sea, where it was eaten by whale.

When the ogre saw that his beloved butterfly rose had gone, he fell sick with grief. An old witch was summoned to cast a spell on him to make him well.

'Make sure he eats plenty of blubber,' said the old witch to the ogre's wife, handing over the bill.

The ogre's wife felt guilty over what she'd done, and

went to her favourite pond to weep. The duck, relaxing on the water, felt sorry for the woman and swam up to her. He offered her a nut that he'd stolen from the butterfly's tree and the ogre's wife smiled through her tears, one of which fell from her cheeks and landed on the duck, turning him into a beautiful Prince.

'Oh, beautiful Prince!' said the ogre's wife. 'If you would do a good deed for me, I would marry you and all my gold and jewels and treasures would be yours.'

'Name the good deed, fair maiden – and it shall be done,' said the Prince.

'I need blubber for my husband, the ogre,' she explained.

The Prince drew his sword and swam off into a tributary,[+] and then to the river, and into the ocean where he met a whale. The whale was the most beautiful he had ever seen, and he fell instantly in love with it. But the whale was sad, because as much as the whale loved the ocean, his dream was to have legs and dance upon the land.

[+] A kind of rivery sort of stream.

The Prince waved his magic sword and when the whale awoke, he was washed up on a beach and, from the waist down, HUMAN! The Prince fell to his knees and proposed marriage and the whale accepted at once.

The ogre's wife saw all this through a secret pendant, and grew as jealous as she'd ever been. She transformed herself into her own husband and tricked the whale and the Prince into having their wedding at her castle.

On their wedding night, though, the ogre's wife snuck into their wedding chamber, stole the Prince's sword and cut the sleeping whale in two. Out of the whale's belly rose the beautiful butterfly rose.

As soon as the Prince saw it, the spell was broken and he turned back into a duck.

The ogre's wife, overcome with happiness, picked up the flower in her hands and took it to her ailing husband. As soon as he saw it, he became well and realised it was his wife he had been in love with all along.

The ogre kissed his wife and the butterfly rose magically turned back into a butterfly again and came to life.

The duck was so happy that everything was as it was that he turned back into the Prince again, and left the castle satisfied that the butterfly had learned his lesson: He who has stones thrown at him had better duck.

Acknowledgements

Many thanks to all those at Hardie Grant Egmont who helped nail this thing together: Hilary Rogers, Marisa Pintado and Penelope White for their gentle guidance and wild encouragement, Pooja Desai for her wonderful design, and Luna Soo for her kind counsel.

To Jonathan Bentley my gratitude for lending this book his considerable talent and bringing so many of the characters and scenes to such vivid life – and for being nice enough not to complain when I asked if the Prince Regent could please look more like Kenneth Williams.

An oblique nod to João de Deus of Abadiânia, Brazil, for prescribing twenty-four hours of solitude in my *pousada* while I was making a documentary about him (I wrote the story about the monkey instead). And finally, a salute beyond the veil to Carlo Collodi (who wrote *Pinocchio*) and Norman Hunter (who wrote *The Incredible Adventures of Professor Branestawm*); two authors whose work I read and re-read as a child and have never forgotten. In fact, I can see the original books sitting up on my bookshelf as I write this, some forty-seven years later – oh yes, and a big hug to Alfred Bestall too.

- Shaun Micallef

Acknowledgements

I too need to thank the wonderful team at Hardie Grant Egmont: Marisa Pintado for taking a chance on me, Penelope White for her patience and encouragement, and to Pooja Desai for her beautiful design.

This truly was a gift of a book for someone who grew up spending hours poring over Arthur Rackham and W. Heath Robinson. So Shaun, I can't thank you enough for your wonderful words and for having the trust to leave me to it, apart from the Kenneth Williams thing.

To my family for their love and support, especially my parents who never told me to get a proper job and particularly my wife Maripaz, who has put up with my locking myself away in my studio for so many hours. I promise we will get out more now.

- Jonathan Bentley